DEATH OF THE WILD BIRD

When Jonathan Blake came to LOHM to find out about revolver shooting, he discovered that the premises were apparently deserted. But he soon found himself locked in — with a dead woman and a man who stood over her with a gun in his hand. But why would a business tycoon murder a wild bird and wreck his whole life? Blake didn't believe that he would, but it is hard to prove innocence when you have seen the end part of the act committed and there is no other person in the building.

JOHN NEWTON CHANCE

DEATH OF THE WILD BIRD

Complete and Unabridged

LINFORD
Leicester

First published in Great Britain in 1968 by
Robert Hale Limited
London

First Linford Edition
published 2002
by arrangement with
Robert Hale Limited
London

British Library CIP Data

Chance, John Newton, *1911 – 1983*
  Death of the wild bird.—Large print ed.—
Linford mystery library
  1. Detective and mystery stories
  2. Large type books
  I. Title
  823.9'14 [F]

ISBN 0–7089–9825–9

Published by
F. A. Thorpe (Publishing)
Anstey, Leicestershire

Set by Words & Graphics Ltd.
Anstey, Leicestershire
Printed and bound in Great Britain by
T. J. International Ltd., Padstow, Cornwall

This book is printed on acid-free paper

**Neath Port Talbot
Libraries
Llyfrgelloedd
Castell-Nedd
Port Talbot**

CHANCE, J.N.
....

Death of the wild bird
....

....

*Books should be returned or renewed by the last date
stamped above.
Dylid dychwelyd llyfrau neu eu hadnewyddu erbyn y
dyddiad olaf a nodir uchod*   **NP56**

1

I had never heard of LOHM until that May when the note came from my old club. At the time I was down in Cornwall at my inherited mansion and thinking of going up to London, where I had kept on my humble suburban mews flat. The club of which I speak was mainly concerned with games, PE, fencing, bowmanship and revolver shooting. The last was the important thing to me as a sport of which I am very fond, the challenge to co-relation between the eye, the brain and the muscle. I have some good guns, and the fact that the note had bad news gloomed me more than a little.

These are the days of the credit world, and what seems like a business empire today can be bust for millions tomorrow. You can't trust the look of anything. The news I had was that owing to staggering overheads and increasing costs in all directions the club had voted itself to close before it was forced to go broke.

Underneath this sad news Jamie, the secretary had written, 'Dear Johnny, advise you to get in touch with LOHM — ' he gave an address in Surrey, ' — who have rapidly become the tops in the sort of thing we tried to do. Expensive, but what isn't? Regards, Jamie.'

It was worth finding out, as pistol clubs are few and very far between.

I went up to London the following day. There was some business with my solicitors who were still disentangling some details of my inheritance. There is also a policeman of whom I am fond because he didn't do me for a naughty business some time back. He is a Chief Superintendent at the yard called Bogey Shifnal, and his favourite pub is the Green Arrow, where we met that day.

We spoke of many things and then it occurred to me he might have heard about LOHM. He had.

'What is it? Sounds like a Swiss engineering group.'

'In fact it stands for League of Heavy

2

Men,' he said, shifting his great weight on his seat.

'Oh, humour.'

'You have to be well in to know it,' Bogey said. 'The customers think it stands for some mystic physical cult, but in fact the club side of the business is genuine. You'll be a right fit there, now the old Greenwich Sun has closed down.'

'Why club side of the business? Is it a cover for another line?'

'Surely. The firm specialises in industrial counter espionage, a very profitable business, but it's getting increasingly dangerous.'

'So I have heard. But you don't hear much on those lines. International espionage seems far more publicised.'

'It's a good set-up because it's very small,' Bogey said, accepting another drink with a nod. 'There is just John Marsh and three beautiful damsels, and I mean beautiful.'

'Really,' I said. 'Who does the physical instruction then?'

'Marsh and the girls. They teach fencing, judo, the lot. They're very popular with the weary businessmen. You don't find any executives there who aren't holding their bellies in till they almost burst.'

'Well, they say a woman can take any job these days,' I said. 'But is that all?'

'There's a cleaning staff, of course, and a couple of typist-secretaries, but the work is done by the four. The whole set-up is ingenious because the class of executive they get to have their muscles toned up are the very ones who would have industrial spy troubles.'

'I see. But is all this generally known?'

'No. It's very close — the espionage part, of course. Spies and counter spies don't go around in sandwich boards, but we know all about it because we deal in knowing about new firms and oddities. Also they have called us in on occasion to clean up after them.'

'Oh, it gets criminal, does it?'

'It gets bloody dangerous,' said Bogey. 'It might suit your evil character in some ways. Have you done anything lately, or are you settling down as a country gentleman?'

'Settling down, mate.'

'You won't settle down till you get some woman to chain you to the legit bedpost. Once you get the bug for getting into trouble like you have, you don't get rid of it. It keeps getting you. I know. I deal with nobody but crooks myself.'

'Thank you.'

I rang LOHM about five that day.

'I'm interested in joining for pistol shooting,' I said. 'Can I come down tomorrow morning and see somebody?'

'Well, it's Saturday, but I expect Mr. Marsh and the others will be here,' a girl said. 'Will you hold on?'

When I had held on a minute and she came back and said it would be all right, anytime after ten.

And that was what started the whole damn thing. At the time it was only a joke for Bogey Shifnal, and even he soon had to stop laughing.

★ ★ ★

It was a fine hot morning. I drove down into Surrey in a new, open Mercedes, a

5

present from an old friend called Gabriel Pachmann, who had stolen my girl in return for me helping him to slaughter a few Caribbean crooks, only a week or two back.

Whatever Bogey said, I was right in the mood to settle down then, for my visit to Shark Island, though lasting only a day, had felt like nine separate lifetimes, and I'm a poor cat.

There wasn't a lot of traffic. Most of it would be late coming out and then parked in the towns, shopping. I got to the grounds of LOHM at about five to ten. I'm one of those anxious types that if somebody says a time, I have to be there.

The building was new, red brick and horizontal steel windows. The sort of thing the architect gets by piling up empty boxes, pushing one a bit this way, and a bit that way, then sticks strips of silver paper on here and there to see what the windows look like and then draws it and gets it built. He also gets paid for it.

The grounds were quite spacious, with a wood one side and farm fields on the other. The lawns were good and there was

6

a man cruising up and down one with a hover type mowing machine.

I didn't look at him, but soon wished I had. I pulled up by the entrance and the mowing motor buzzed out of sight round a line of brilliant rhododendron bushes up near the road.

The main doors were swing double glass ones with a few brass studs so you could just see there was something there.

They swung in easily, so somebody was in.

I thought.

There wasn't a sound inside the building. Nothing at all. I had the feeling that it was dead empty.

I walked down the spacious corridor. Not a sound. I shoved a button in the wall marked 'Enquiries' and there was a buzz in the silence, then nothing again. Nobody came.

Yet as I went on I sniffed the wretched acrid stink of a cigarette left to burn itself. It came from an open door on the left marked 'John Marsh'. Inside smoke rose from an ash-tray on a desk by a telephone that was unhooked and lying by an open diary.

I went in. The cigarette had burnt down about a half-inch by itself and I stubbed it. There was a small, fine china cup with coffee in it. The coffee was hot.

Then the phone spoke and almost made me jump.

'I have that call for you now,' a woman said.

I lifted the phone.

'Continental Exchange. Your call to Perpignan.'

'The man's gone out. I can't find anybody here.'

'Oh? But we were only three minutes getting through. Surely he would have waited?'

'One would think so. But he didn't.'

'I'd better cancel.'

'Yes. He'll call you again.'

Three minutes. Three minutes of burning fag, hot coffee. The dead sure signs that Marsh or somebody had been there three minutes before.

I went out into the corridor and bellowed. My own voice came back. The corridor angled to a glass garden door on the left. It was unlocked and I went out and shouted. Nobody answered. The mower had stopped buzzing. There were birds singing over in the tall trees of the wood beyond the garden but no other sound.

The idea that something was wrong was strong in me, but one often gets notions like that and puts it down to a sense of the over-dramatic. I shoved double doors at the end of the corridor and went into a magnificent gymnasium, everything of the latest, everything of the best, a great hall with two-inch pine floor, polished like glass. Yet it wasn't slippery, for I tried it as a test for common sense in the architect. As an erstwhile surveyor I sometimes think they haven't got much.

At quarter past ten the feeling of wrongness had got so strong that I stopped wandering up and down the corridor and decided to have a look round.

There were a couple more private offices, with girls' names on, and a secretaries' office with electric typewriters, photo-copiers, tapes, filing cabinets, the lot.

On the other side there was a splendid bar as good as in any top flight hotel and big double-glazed windows looking out to the gardens.

There was a drink standing on the bar counter, a lager, frothy and still working its bubbles from the bottom.

At the end of the corridor, facing the garden door was an unlocked door marked 'Private'. It was a flat, as modern and luxurious as the rest of the outfit, and as empty.

Up the wide stairs there was another flat, door ajar. It was a woman's flat, beautiful and empty. There was a second flat next door, also open to the view, also empty. This, too, looked like a woman's flat, or a very untidy girl's flat, everything left everywhere. This one looked, more than the others, as if the owner had rushed out, just dropping everything.

Or as if she had been dragged out in the middle of doing several things at once. The third flat was locked. I rang the bell but nobody came. I didn't expect they would. I was sure by then that the place was empty.

Downstairs again I went into Marsh's office, took one of his cigarettes from the desk box and wondered what to do.

The place was like the *Marie Celeste*, suddenly abandoned, within minutes of someone discovering the empty hulk.

But what to do? The owners might have had a sudden, urgent and honest reason for running out, leaving everything. My naturally dishonest mind couldn't think of one.

The same silence held downstairs as up and outside in the garden. Dead. This weird emptiness was the last atmosphere one would expect in an up-to-the-minute go-ahead firm like this.

I just didn't believe they would all four have fled the place in one explosion of panic. After all, what monster could have appeared at that time in the morning and scared them into a headlong bolt?

All I could think of was they had been gassed and kidnapped a couple of minutes before I got there. That wasn't likely, either.

But that phone call. Marsh wouldn't have gone out when he knew the exchange would call back in a couple of minutes.

So I did the only thing I could think of. I went out to find that gardener.

His machine was behind the last bush, but he had gone. His battered old felt hat lay upturned on the grass nearby as if it had fallen off as he ran.

A car went by on the road. When it had gone the silence fell again. Even the birds seemed to have stopped. They started again as I walked back to the building, as if glad I was going back.

* * *

When I got into the hallway again I heard somebody talking. It came from down near Marsh's office. I ran down there, making little noises in case the voice stopped.

It was coming from Marsh's office. I stopped at the door.

It was the phone again. It was lying on the desk though I had shoved it back on the hooks after answering the exchange.

A quick look round showed everything else as before and still no one about.

'Look here, Marsh,' the voice said, 'I suggest you take another look at the whole thing. Get a new angle. The old one isn't going to work. Don't you agree?'

There was a silence.

'Yes, I thought you would,' the voice went on. 'So we'll re-think the whole business. When will you come up?'

Another silence.

'Yes. Thursday will be fine. Yes. 'Bye, then.'

I know nothing of telephone circuits, so I couldn't tell if Marsh had been speaking on some junction line to this one. If he had, then how hadn't I heard him?

The only thing to do I did. I picked up the phone and called.

'Mr. Marsh. I am Jonathan Blake.'

All I got was the dialling buzz.

For the second time I replaced the machinery. It showed that somebody was around, somebody hiding, or somebody out to impress me with tricks.

After all, the voice had paused for Marsh's answers, and so do actors carrying on the one side act with a phone. There was nothing mysterious about that.

The only mystery was why the hell anybody should bother to do it at all.

Then I noticed that the desk diary was shut. I hadn't bothered to look at it before; in fact, I have a thing about looking at other people's diaries as I should have a strong thing about them prying into mine.

But this small item seemed to have some meaning, and I opened it again at the day's date.

There it said, 'Jonathan Blake, 10 a.m.'

Then I heard somebody in the corridor outside, and went out to face the comer.

It was a postman about to knock at the secretary's door.

'There's nobody in,' I said.

'I'll just leave them,' he said. 'Never much on Saturday.'

'Are you always as late as this?'

'Sure. It's the end of my round. But I only come on Saturdays. One of the girls

14

collects from the Office ordinary days. Funny there's nobody here at all. There's usually somebody about.'

'You always see someone?'

'Always. Are you waiting?'

'Yes. It's strange nobody being here. What sort of a lot are they?'

'Oh, very nice people. Pleasant, businesslike, I should say, too. It's funny nobody's here. Everything open, like.'

'They live here?'

'Oh yes. There's four flats here. Well, I suppose I'll leave these in the office.'

He opened the secretary door.

'You knocked,' I said. 'Is there usually somebody in that office on Saturday mornings?'

'Sometimes. I always leaves everything in here.'

He put the mail on a table by the door and looked round as if somebody might pop out from somewhere. Then he nodded.

'Hope somebody turns up for you,' he said.

'Thanks.' I watched him through the glass doors. He got into his van and drove away out into the road.

Then I looked through the letters. There was one with the postmark Perpignan. I felt a terrific urge to open it and put it down before temptation got the better of me.

If there was something wrong in this place, then whoever was responsible had made a good move already. I had given my name over the phone, thus proving I was the geezer expected at 10 a.m.

It was then about ten-forty and I had an idea. I went back into Marsh's office and wrote in large letters on his note block: 'Back at twelve noon. Blake.'

Then I went out, whistling. I drove along until I came to a village a mile down the road. There was a first-class hostelry standing back of a smooth green, with a soft, rich-looking church beside it. The cottages and houses were all fine. It was a Surrey show place.

No one was in the lounge bar but a man in jacket and breeches and stock who was packing a shelf with cigarettes. I ordered a drink and he was affable about the fine weather and chances for sport that weekend.

'Do you know John Marsh?' I said.

'For sure,' he said. 'They have the place up the road. Rather splendid gymnasium type place.'

'Yes. I've just called there. I had an appointment at ten, but nobody was there at all. But nobody.'

'Nobody?' he said, staring. 'But there's always somebody. John makes a point. There is always somebody.'

'He makes a point, does he?'

'Absolutely. Positively. There is always someone on duty watch. They have pretty wide connections. Overseas and all. They're not too keen on the automatics for answering. Don't know why. Seem all right to me.'

Obviously the landlord knew nothing of the espionage connections. He thought it was all gymwise business.

It seemed he was Commander Hopkins and gave some details of the habits of the four operators at LOHM. The three girls were Sheila, Mary and Jane, and were all in their twenties, the Commander said, and were some special tarties, the

Commander also said. He said he wouldn't be able to work with a bevy like that without going mad with lust. It sounded all right.

But LOHM was all wrong.

He kept coming back to it.

'You sure there's nobody there?' He repeated it incredulously.

'It's quiet as a morgue. In fact, for the first five minutes I thought it was one.'

'Don't grasp it at all. Everything shipshape there?'

'Tidy as a tomb.'

'I wonder what the hell could have happened? I mean, he's so fixed on that somebody always being there.'

'Look,' I said, 'when I got there he had a cigarette burning in an ash-tray and a hot cup of coffee. Now what do you think would have made him run out?'

'That's ruddy queer,' he said, frowning harder than before. 'Ruddy queer. I mean, I used to joke about them taking duty watch and that. No, they wouldn't all go out. Perhaps some kind of alarm went off.'

'What kind of alarm?'

'Damned if I know. Can't think of one.'

The important thing was his view of the emptiness of LOHM. A thing never heard of, but what had been constantly heard of was Marsh's intention that it should not be left.

My drink finished, I wished him farewell.

'You going back?' he said curiously.

'Eventually,' I said. 'Not before twelve.'

'I wonder whether to ring up,' he said.

'No,' I said. 'There's nobody to answer. If it's the same at twelve, I'll be back.'

I drove back fast and pulled into a track that ran into the woods. I left the Merc there, then went through the wood and climbed the fence dividing the wood from LOHM's vegetable garden. Once over it I ran as quietly as I could.

The glass side door was still unfastened. I went in. If anybody was about they would be caught now, for the time was eleven-fifteen.

I stopped at the corner and looked along the empty corridor to the glass main doors. Instinctively rather than sensibly, I felt somebody was there now, and started to walk up the corridor, making a row with my shoes on the floor.

A man came out of Marsh's office. He stared at me.

'Seen Mr. Marsh?' he said. 'Don't seem to be nobody about.'

'Who are you?'

'I doos the garden. Come for my pay Saturday.'

'Do you come full time?'

'Five days.' He nodded.

'Not Saturday?'

'Not Saturday, no. On Saturday I doos the buying. Anything wanted. Always comes about now and there's my money and any fer what's wanted.'

'Wanted for the garden, that is?'

'Yes. I gets a cut. Perks.'

'Your lawn mower is up amongst the bushes there,' I said.

He looked round to the main doors, startled.

'Her shouldn't be there. Somebody must a used it.'

'Somebody was using it at ten o'clock this morning.'

'Well, it's theirs if they wants to use it,

but I keep them lawns trim. I don't see that anybody would want to cut another swathe off there now.'

He was angry at the thought somebody had criticised his work. He seemed a genuine gardener.

'Was your money left anywhere?'

'I can't find anybody. Very strange, that. Always somebody here.' He scratched his face. 'Well, I s'pose I'd better get on. Wife's waiting out in the car.'

'What'll you do about your money?'

'I got enough to get on. I'll be here Monday.'

He walked off and out of the doors. A battered Mini pick-up truck swung away from somewhere by the house side, went to the entrance gates and vanished behind the road hedge.

There was no sign of anybody else, and no sign that anybody else had been there since I had gone. I looked through the ground floor rooms and offices once more. Everything was the same as I had seen it before, except the lager on the bar counter had gone flat as ditchwater.

Once again in my undesirable solitude,

but backed now with the opinions of three who knew the Lohmers, I decided it was up to me to do something.

It was no longer possible to accept this situation as free of any menace. Something was wrong, and I kidded myself it was my duty as a citizen to find out what. That was as good an excuse as any for my uncontrollable nosiness.

But I didn't ring the police because that seemed out of proportion to the situation.

I went into the bar and held the lager glass up to the light. The rim of the glass was gold, but I made out a lipstick smear on it. In a place like this, a dirty glass was unthinkable, so I put this one down to an interrupted lady drinker.

That done, I had a drink myself. The silence, which had been tense at the start, was now depressing. Yet I had the feeling that soon, somebody would come in. Why, I have no idea. Perhaps the neglected lager was some kind of vicarious company.

I assumed there were no cellars, as I had seen fuel oil filling valves outside the house. So that the only place I had not seen into was the locked flat.

Somewhere around the place there must be keys. I went out of the bar and tried the secretaries' office. There was a bunch of keys which I went up and tried, with no luck.

I went into two other offices which belonged to Mary and Jane. Sheila did not seem to have one. She, I was to learn, ran the bar and catering.

Just opening and slamming drawers took a while and all I got from it was the odd information that none were locked. In view of the fact that LOHM dealt in secrets, then somewhere around there was some kind of hidden safe deposit, where current papers were kept.

It was around ten minutes to twelve when I went once more into Marsh's office. I opened and slammed drawers and found no keys. Then I sat down in his chair and just looked round the room.

I saw no safes. It was a fine room, luxurious. You knew it was an office because it had three telephones on the vast desk and other small equipment. Otherwise it was all big chairs and a settee big enough for table tennis.

The room had a kind of wall decoration of vertical flutes which could have hidden a dozen wall-safes. It would have been a waste of time to look.

The phone went and I answered with a kind of excitement inside me like a wound-up spring.

But a voice said: 'Is that the book-makers?'

For a while I wondered if the house keys were kept in one of the open flats, but knowing my luck that morning I thought that if so, it was probably in the locked one.

So I went up the stairs again and looked at the plain sapele door and the expensive, solid furniture and the mortice lock and pondered the possibility of picking it.

That illegal thought brought it home to me I was wasting my time playing detectives. Whatever had happened was no affair of mine. I had no business with LOHM. I had merely thought of it to shoot pistols in and made an arrangement to call. What on earth was I doing, wandering around the place as if this could be some tragedy, and could be mine?

Common sense was returning. It had been an enthralling morning, thinking and playing around. It was enthralling still, but it just wasn't my mystery.

So I got up and laughed and pushed the damn door I couldn't find a key for and it just went wide open.

I remember standing there, but not what I felt, for I knew it had been locked before and that someone had unlocked it recently.

I went to the door and looked in. The same riches were evident in the furnishings and fittings, though to an inexperienced eye it could have looked almost plain.

I went in, thinking that whoever had unlocked the door had been on the inside of it.

Then the door slammed behind me and the key clicked in the lock.

I am always a sucker for a kid's

joke. Only to take the childishness off it, there was a dead girl lying with her head just sticking out of the open door to the lounge, a couple of feet away from me.

2

She lay there with her head sticking out of the doorway, eyes wide in surprise, looking at the ceiling. A pretty girl, with fair, tossed hair. As I moved closer, I could see she was naked.

Beyond her painted toenails the room spread out on a plain blue carpet. The man stood by the broad window. He just stood there, looking at me blankly, a gun still hanging from his hand.

He was a big, baggy sort of man, heavy-featured, with untidy red hair and bright green eyes, dull now as if in some kind of blank surprise. His white shirt was undone at the collar and his tie loosed and twisted to one side as if he had felt hot — or choking.

I had the feeling I had seen him before, but it was a vague sense and feelings like that can cheat.

The man realised he held the gun in his hand and raised it. But instead of pointing it at me, or even at himself — a possibility that struck me then — he just tossed it into the seat of a deep arm-chair.

Then he stuffed his hands into his pockets and stared through me.

'Why in hell did I do that?' he said, gruffly.

'Don't ask me,' I said. I knelt by the girl to see if she was right dead.

She was. Shot between the breasts, and from the quiet, almost puzzled look on her face I should have guessed death must have struck her without her having had time to feel anything.

I got up. The man didn't look like a killer, but you never can tell when passion comes into anything.

'We'd better call some policemen, hadn't we?' I said.

He kept his hands in his pockets and just shrugged his shoulders. I went to a phone behind the chair where the gun was. It was dead. The line ran into the skirting all right, so it must have been cut somewhere beyond that.

The man just stood there watching me as if I was some part of a dream he was having. I picked up the gun in my handkerchief and took it with me to look for another phone.

There were two more. One in the bedroom and one in the kitchen. All dead men. I went back into the hall and tried the door which had been shut on me. It was locked from the other side. It had a mortice lock and needed a key.

Back in the room the man had sat on a long settee by the window and appeared to be staring out at the countryside.

'We're locked in with a battery of dead phones,' I said. 'Every window in the place is double-glazed, burglar-proof stuff. Nobody could get in. Nobody can get out without a key. You must have it.'

I held out a hand. He stared up to me.

'The key?' he said blankly.

'The key to the flat,' I said. 'Come on! There's a lot to be done!'

'I haven't got a key to this place,' he rumbled.

He still had a dreamlike attitude, very odd and his voice was all on a level, as if nothing mattered much at all.

'How did you get in?' I said, impatiently.

'She let me in.'

'Who is she?'

'Sheila. She lives here,' he said.

'One of the firm!'

'Well, she entertains the men customers,' he said, looking past me to the corpse. 'Or she did.'

'Do you mean they've got a brothel attached for the weary executive?' I said incredulously.

He shrugged again. I took a keener look round the room. There was a silk dressing gown tossed over the arm of a chair. It looked as if the girl had taken it off and girls who parade in the nude before tired businessmen are likely to be loose —

It was the tired businessman that hooked up in my memory. I looked round at the man again.

'Are you Geoffrey Caswell that was, now Lord Kilgallen?'

He stared up at me and frowned.

'Yes,' he said slowly. 'I should say that.'

'You would say that?' I repeated. 'Are

30

you dopey with shock? Are you Kil-gallen?'

'Yes.'

He shoved a hand into the breast pocket of his big, loose jacket and pulled out a cigarette case. He took one out and tossed it to me, then had one himself.

It was a situation that required a quiet smoke. This man was in command of one of the largest industrial concerns in the country. Produce ranging from transistors to locomotives poured out from his many bellied interests. But he knew more than administration, finance and management; he was a technician. One of the rare birds who knew the production industry personally and had come to manage through the shops. And still a man of no more than forty-five. A man at the top, a millionaire in money and in brain power.

Here, sitting on a sofa, dumb as a coot, looking at a tart he had just shot.

I don't know where the idea of the tragic matched up in me, perhaps it was the idea of a great man throwing the lot down the drain for a morning frig. It seemed out of all proportion. It was. But it wasn't uncommon, either. People did things like that.

It was unpleasant and surprising that it should turn out to be Kilgallen tripped up into a sordid mess.

It was the same to find that LOHM, so respectable and efficient should have whores on the staff to amuse the executives.

To shake off a short feeling of depression at these findings I went out to the door again and banged on it hard. I made a good row and shouted, and there was no answer.

Then I went round the flat again, but there was no way out but another door at the back, also fixed with a mortice lock needing a key or a very good picker.

The windows did not open. The whole place was air-conditioned, and everything double-glazed to keep uneven temperature out and noise out as well. It also kept noise in.

The grounds were still deserted, so I had no need to feel frustrated that I wouldn't be heard shouting if anyone had been there.

As I turned back from the fire escape door by the kitchen Kilgallen came up. He looked different now. As if he had woken up.

'I killed that girl!' he said, incredulously.

'You did.'

'But why in hell did I do that?' he shouted and pushed his fingers through his hair. 'I've never seen her before in my ruddy life!'

'You don't have to — that sort,' I said.

'Look Mr. Marsh — ' he said urgently.

'Hi, just a minute!' I stopped him. 'I'm not Marsh. I'm here to see Marsh.'

'Then who in hell are you?' he said blankly.

'Look,' I said, 'we seem to be trapped in here *pro tem*. Sit down there. Let's straighten this a bit. I feel a little twisted in the head. Why did you come?'

'I had an appointment to see Mr. Marsh.'

'At what time?'

'Ten.'

'This gets crazier. I had an appointment with Marsh at ten.'

'Impossible,' he said. 'They couldn't cock things up like that.'

'When did you make the appointment?'

'Yesterday afternoon. On the phone.'

'Me too. What time did you get here this morning?'

'I was early. The chauffeur boobed with the time. About twenty to, I suppose. He's a new chap. Takes time running them in.'

I sat on the table and watched him.

'You went into the bar and had a drink.'

He nodded.

'Who served you?'

'Nobody. When I got in here a voice came over the Tannoy, asking me to wait in the bar and help myself.'

'What sort of voice?'

'A girl's voice.'

'So you poured a lager.'

'How do you know?' His eyes were bright and shrewd now. Even with a dead weight on his mind there was a twinkle somewhere in them.

'I'm guessing. You go on.'

'The voice came through again and

34

said Marsh was up in flat four if I would go up there. I came up and the door opened just when I got to it. The girl was there in a dressing gown. I said I thought there had been a mistake, but she said No and stood back for me to go in.'

He breathed a bit hard now, as if anger was rising.

'Well, I got into that lounge and she slipped the gown off. I was dead lost. When I come on a business appointment that kind of thing is a shock. In the morning, bright daylight — it was all idiotic somehow. I'm no prude, but it seemed most ludicrous . . .

'Then she started talking about pictures — '

He stopped and took a long breath.

'Before we go any further, did you come to arrange a physical improvement course?'

'Yes,' he said.

'But that wasn't all?'

'Look here, Mr. — '

I told him my name.

'You can trust me,' I said. 'I've had troubles myself in the past. Also, you've

35

bloody well got to.'

'Yes. It was to do with business.'

'And she started talking about pictures. What pictures? Screw type?'

'The whole thing began to look like a blackmail set-up. She in the nude and everything.'

'Did you think she meant you were both being photographed then?'

'I don't know about that, but she said she had some prints there.'

'Did you see them?'

'No.'

'You shot her first?'

He didn't answer but stared through me and showed his teeth. Then, after a while, he said, 'Yes.'

'There's something wrong here,' I said. 'But get on. Did you bring a gun?'

'Of course not! Why on earth should I carry a gun around?'

'It was lying there ready for you?'

'It was on the coffee table.'

'But were you angry? Did you see red or what?'

'I was numb,' he said. 'Numb. I suppose it was shock or something. There was this primitive reaction.'

'Extremely primitive,' I said. 'A man like you, used to considering a thousand details to every process, a thousand possibilities to every risk, go and shoot the girl without thinking that she obviously couldn't have been working alone.'

'I didn't think at all.'

'For the first time in your life, obviously.'

'You're too kind.' He grinned briefly.

'She said she had the pictures,' I said.

'Yes. But I didn't see them.'

'Let's look around. They must have been somewhere handy.'

'How could there be any?' he protested as he followed me out of the kitchen. 'I don't go in for that kind of thing.'

'She must have had some,' I said.

At this time I was thinking of LOHM as efficient if, as now was very clear, damned evil. It didn't sound the sort of set-up that would say something existed if it didn't.

We found a set of big prints in a drawer in a polished table in the lounge. They were shockers. And they all featured the dead girl and Kilgallen.

I saw his eyes almost glowing with fury or shock or something indescribable.

'They're fakes!' he cried.

'But that is you, isn't it?'

'It looks like it. But I never saw that girl before in my life!'

'It's you in every one of them, isn't it?'

'It looks like it!' he shouted. 'But it isn't! They must have dubbed my head on. Unless I'm a sleepwalker, and I don't believe anybody could go through these performances in his sleep!'

'These weren't posed,' I said. 'They're action pictures taken by an expert. The performers don't seem to know he was there.'

'Sex!' he said. 'But this is sex extraordinary. I've never even thought — Good God! Where are the negatives? If this lot got out — Who'd believe they were faked to be me?'

I took the pictures to the light and looked at the man's figure in all the frames. You couldn't see where the head had been scrubbed off and Kilgallen's put on. I put them down on the table.

'I should say it was you,' I said.

'I tell you it's a fake!'

'It was a very expert photographer who did that job,' I said. 'A professional. I should say a man used to doing a lot of advertising photography, cutting in, painting out, superimposing. Anyone not doing this sort of thing from long experience would be bound to bodge it. That is my guess. But it won't help you. If these pictures have been shunted around I should say you've had it.'

★   ★   ★

'They're bad enough for me to have shot her?' he said. 'People will think that, won't they?'

'Yes, they'll think that. They might say you were afraid these would get back to your wife amongst other things.'

'I'm not married,' he said, abruptly.

'Not married?' It hit me stupid. Why on earth would anybody try this kind of blackmail picture on an unmarried man?

'No.'

'But I don't see what the point is, then!'

'They would discredit me. In fact, I'd say they'd finish me as far as I'm concerned now. This kind of smear — if you can call it as light as that — would have a very bad effect. I have a board of directors and thousands of shareholders. They may be broadminded, but would you trust your all to someone who — indulged in this kind of thing?'

I got out my cigarettes.

'You know better than I do,' I said.

'What the hell am I going to do?' he said. 'My chauffeur out there will know I'm here — '

'There's no chauffeur outside. No car out there but mine.'

'No?' He stared. 'Then where the hell is he?'

'Don't ask me.'

I went back to the flat door and banged again, without any result. The phones were tried once more and stayed dead. I even had a go at the front door lock with a metal skewer. I could have saved my efforts.

Early in the proceedings Kilgallen had taken a bedcover and put it over the girl, but even so I kept my eyes well away from that sickening mound on the mat.

'Can't we smash a window?' he said.

'They look like half-inch plate, double,' I said. 'But I suspect they're tougher than that. I understand there are reasons why this building might need to be a fortress on account of what secrets it might hold on occasion.'

'I'm shattered by the whole bloody business!' he shouted. 'I came to do business. I have had this firm checked and it was a first-class result. First-class!'

'I heard well of it, too. But the espionage work was covered by the gymnasium front. Perhaps a third activity was hidden by the second. Whatever the reports were, these things have happened. You were tricked. So was I. I was sealed up in here with you. What in blazes was the point of that?'

He marched about the room. 'What possessed me?' he said. 'I must have gone off my head!'

'You saw nobody but the girl?'

'No.'

'She led you in here and threatened you with disaster, leaving a gun on the table between you. The girl must have been off her head as well.' I looked at him pacing up and down furiously. 'Are you sure the gun was there?'

He stopped and turned and pointed to the table.

'It was there,' he said. 'Where else would I have got it?'

'It's a low table,' I said. 'You had to bend. You're pretty big, so you bent. Then you straightened up and blazed away.'

'I don't remember doing that, one doesn't. In a rage these things are hardly noticed. As you say, I must have bent to get the ruddy thing. My God! with every minute that passes the harder it gets to believe this is me, here in this damned room!'

'I should say in your position you're a man to overwork a good deal,' I said.

'You have to push it pretty hard,' he said, and started to walk again.

'Have you ever had a breakdown?'

He stopped, turned and looked at me.

'There was one. A couple of years back. I took a three months' rest.'

'What kind of a bust was it?'

'Couldn't sleep. Nervous dyspepsia. Depression. All quite usual. The main drag is that life gets dreamlike, and you don't judge things properly. If a problem comes up you decide anything, to get it out of the way quickly. You get worried you'll let yourself go. The point is, you get to a pitch where you're not sure you won't let yourself go.'

'So you had treatment.'

'They put me to sleep for three days. Then I had a lot of fresh air and exercise and regular meals and a psychiatrist — '

Suddenly he chucked himself on to the settee and looked at me. 'Right from the time you came in, I've been wondering if they'll go back to that.'

'They're bound to. It will tie in with the sudden rage and shooting,' I said. 'But what's the problem? You shot her, didn't you? You don't want to disprove that?'

'I'm not thinking straight,' he said. 'My head's a kind of fuzz. The whole thing's a shatterer.'

43

'You were an agent,' I said. 'Somebody wanted the girl dead. They fixed you to do it.'

'Knowing of my weakness,' he said dully.

'Weakness? There's no weakness about overdoing things and having to take time off to cool. You have the wrong angle. Or have you, at the back of your mind, the idea that you're barmy and you're frightened somebody might notice it?'

He burst into a sudden short laugh.

'You have a way of putting things,' he said. 'There are two answers to a good question. The first is: no, when I'm sane. The second is: yes, when I'm overworked up.'

'You're not married. Do you live with a woman?'

'No. I was married at one time. It failed because I was lost in my work. She was left alone too much and there's always a man with less work on his hands.'

'Is she alive?'

'Yes. I haven't seen her for a while this time, but we meet quite often. Jill and I are still fond of each other but you can't expect a woman to run second fiddle all the time.'

He got up and tried the phone again. Dead.

'What in hell will I do?' he said, in despair.

'You can't do anything until we get out of here,' I said.

'Somebody must come soon,' he said.

'I don't know about that,' I said. 'This is, after all, the revered weekend, an institution rarely ignored. It could well be that LOHM have chosen this weekend to take off. After all, those are the signs.'

'Why make appointments with you and me?' he demanded.

'What time did you make yours?'

'About five. My secretary would know.'

'You didn't speak?'

'No. Marsh wasn't there, I understood.'

'That's funny. I understood he was. Perhaps our times are further apart than you think, though. So your secretary spoke to a secretary here?'

'Yes.'

I went round the flat and looked out of the windows. There wasn't a soul in sight.

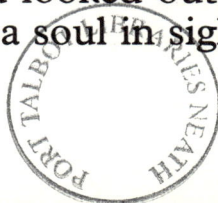

Far off, on a hill I saw a tractor, small as a pin, spreading lime, judging from the clouds drifting behind it. Otherwise there were just a few rooks circling over some elms on the other side of the farm fields.

In a kitchen cupboard I found a tool-box containing a pound of two-inch nails, a pair of pincers and a medium hammer.

I hit the inner pane of the kitchen window and the hammer came back so springily it almost broke my wrist.

'Bullet proof,' I said. I spoke to myself for he was brooding on the vast settee in the lounge.

There was a lot of food in the cupboards and the built-in fridge. I had already found a cabinet with a lot of drink in the lounge. We could last the weekend with every modern con., but what if nobody came back then?

Back in the lounge I got a drink. He watched me but did nothing else. 'We'll have to get that girl out of here,' he said huskily.

'All of us,' I said. With a drink on its way down I put the glass on the table then bent and lifted the corner of the bedcover to see her face. 'You sure you don't know her?'

'Positive. Do you?'

'No. She's a good plump birdie.' I felt rotten and let the sheet fall back. 'Poor devil. Just one shot. It could have gone anywhere.'

'Bad luck,' he said.

I got the gun, unwrapped my handkerchief and had a good look. An Italian job with LOHM engraved on the butt. I wouldn't have given it a flick for accuracy. It was a stopper. You kept the trigger squeezed and everything banged off until the last one went.

The magazine had one round gone.

'You must have had a shock when you felt the gun fire and eased your finger,' I said.

'I don't really know what happened.' He looked out of the window, then stood up and shouted. 'Doesn't anybody ever come near this bloody place?'

'You sure that damn gun was on this table?'

'Where else could it have been? I must

have spotted it suddenly and shot off my rocker. I can't think why in hell I did it! I must be mad. It's gone too far. They say when it gets far on you just motor off as the idiot need for immediate safety kicks you in the back. That's it. It was all explained to me.'

There is a danger with explaining all these things to broody types that they will eventually let it get hold of them and they'll do the very thing they were warned against.

But how a man as busy as Kilgallen could have got into a broody state I couldn't think. To be a real brooder you need a lot of time, a lot of nothing to do. He didn't fill the requirements.

The whole thing was mad. That a widey-world girl like Sheila could have blackmailed a big business man with a loaded gun lying in between them was as mad as anything I could joke up.

Unless she thought it was unloaded. If she thought that, a third person in the flat must have loaded it. Where was any third? Kilgallen hadn't seen anybody, or heard anyone.

But it had to be remembered he had been in a state and his evidence on sharp points might be valueless.

Quite valueless. With the madness of the situation I had overlooked an important matter. Timing.

'You don't make sense,' I said. 'You say you came here, took a lager, was told to come up and the girl let you in. You then talked a while. How long?'

He shrugged.

'I don't know. Five minutes. Could be.'

'I got here a couple of minutes after you, wandered around for about forty-five minutes. Then I went down to the pub in the village, had a drink, came back, came up here and found you having just shot the girl.'

He stared.

'No!' he said. 'I couldn't have talked that long. Impossible.'

'Then there's a large slab of time mislaid somewhere. Where? I study the time theories a bit, but I don't see ninety minutes of a bright Saturday morning slipping out and vanishing like that.'

'Are you sure about the time you arrived?'

'I'm never wrong on appointments. It's a nervous disease caused by a strict nurse when I was very small. You, on the other hand, have got into the way of having appointments made for you, and being brought to them on time.'

'There wouldn't be a mistake of ninety minutes!' he protested. 'And you found the lager down there.'

'There is a lot of lager down there. A lot of glasses, too. And there's a small point confusion made me forget. It was a girl drinking that beer.'

'Really, Mr. Blake! My staff couldn't have made a time error that big. In any case, what was I doing during that time? Sleeping?'

'Where were you before you got here?'

'In the car.'

'Just sitting there looking out?'

'No. I was going through papers.'

'Let me go further for you. You were going through papers of a secret nature belonging to your company. You were bringing them here to hand to Mr. Marsh in order to get his help on a matter of some spying going on in your establishments.'

'Yes.'

'Then where are those precious papers? You must have held them close to you. You must have brought them here as you thought Marsh was here. Where are they?'

'My brief-case — ' he said, and pushed his fingers through his hair again. 'I can't remember — '

'Somebody else does,' I suggested.

3

'I must have brought that damn case here,' Kilgallen said, staring round as if he were not quite sure what he was looking for.

'Don't you remember?'

'Not precisely. No. When I saw that girl it took my mind off. It was a shock.'

'But what did you feel before that?'

'Hot. Tired.'

'You've been overdoing it again at the office,' I said.

'I told you, you have to push it. You can't let it push you.'

'You had a lot on your mind when you were coming here for the appointment with Marsh?'

'I had. Yes.'

'So you really didn't take a lot of immediate notice of things when you got here?'

'I was sorting things out in my mind. Getting the facts marshalled. I never like to waste time at an interview. Fumbling for facts is a bad thing. But normally I notice more than I did today. The chauffeur's timing must have upset me.'

'Let us look for that case,' I said.

We went through the flat, looked into cupboards and drawers. It was a girl's flat all right, and a girl with a lot of clothes. There were a lot of magazines in the bedroom, different magazines, odd dates, but each one having the same girl on the cover.

'Who's the model, then?' I said. 'It isn't that poor kid out there.'

'What does it matter?' he said.

We searched the place in all the spots big enough to hold a fat brief-case and did not find it.

'I must have brought it in,' he said. 'Whatever sort of haze I was in I wouldn't have let it go.'

Back in the lounge I took another gulp at my beer. It was very good, and made me realise how warm and dry I was.

'The haze you were in,' I said. 'What put that phrase into your mind?'

He shrugged.

'Did you have any similar feeling to the sense of unreality you had before the breakdown?' I said.

'Yes,' he said, bringing it out with sudden force. 'Yes, I did! It frightened me. Right at this moment I can't afford to break down. It comes right at an important phase in the affairs of my organisation.'

He clearly held back anything that might reveal what that phase was.

'I don't want to know,' I said. 'I'm not interested in your business. Only in your predicament.'

'My predicament is very like yours,' he pointed out. 'We're both locked in here and if you're right, we shan't get out till Monday.'

Again he seemed to bite something back.

'Would that be too late for your business affairs?' I said.

'It would be a day too late,' he said.

It clued me to the fact that he was arranging some tie-up with a Continental interest, for they have a habit of doing things on a Sunday.

'I was just thinking this lock-in could be a means of keeping you away from some appointment. But why the murder complication?'

'I suppose to tie me up completely. You must admit if I fail to turn up tomorrow, and then there follows a publication in certain quarters of those pictures, my credit will be gone, even if the girl wasn't dead, which she is.'

'You're quite sure you never saw her before?'

'Certain.'

'But you might have done, at a restaurant, in a crowded office, at a shareholders' meeting.'

'I usually remember faces.'

'But there are times when we don't,' I said. 'Such as under a drug treatment.'

He stared.

'Well, that's possible, of course. Are you suggesting she could have been at the nursing home?'

'I'm suggesting she could have been seen with you though you may not have seen her. The importance of the point is that it doesn't matter whether you consciously saw her so long as other witnesses saw you together.'

'Hell! Yes!' he grunted. 'I will have a drink after all. I'm getting panicky. Why can't we get out of this damn place?'

'It's been selected as our prison because it is proof against break-ins or outs without a lot of tools, which we haven't got. When the LOHM people had this place built they could have had an idea of some situation such as now.'

He gulped down a Scotch as if he had a grudge against it.

'I can't believe a firm with such a good rating could be a crowd of crooks underneath,' he said.

'I keep wondering that,' I said. 'But what's on the other hand? Nothing. They have a name for never leaving the place. Yet this weekend they do it.'

He banged his glass on the table.

'But why kill one of themselves? It was rigged so that I might kill her, and I damned well did!' He bit that off, too, and turned his back to look out of the windows. His big shoulders sagged as if all his strength was flowing out of him.

'Thieves do fall out,' I said. 'Getting rid of one and you at the same stroke could be counted economical if nothing else.'

'How the hell did I lose my head like that?' he shouted suddenly. 'How did I get into a state of panic that I could have shot a girl down?'

'In such a state how the hell did you hit her?' I said. 'To me, as some sort of marksman, that's a most interesting point. Have you shot revolvers before?'

'No. I'll be quite honest, I've never had anything to do with firearms.'

This brought an interesting thought into my mind. I got the gun, still in my handkerchief and showed him the weapon.

'Which is the safety catch?' I said.

He stared at it.

'I don't know, but as an engineer I'd say it would have to be that catch there. There isn't anything else.'

'But you must have flipped it up to fire.' I watched his puzzled frown. 'You don't remember doing that?'

He wiped his hand down his face, then shook his head. 'I don't remember firing, even. I was as far gone as that.'

'But the girl was looking at you,' I said. 'Didn't she say anything — plead? Make any move to stop you?'

He began to frown as if he began to remember something.

'She said, 'Fire! Fire it! I dare you!'' He stared at me incredulously. 'That's what she said!'

'She dared you to shoot her, knowing the gun was loaded?' I said. 'Knowing she'd just threatened to blackmail you into the gutter? Did she also show you how to unset the safety catch? That's just as insane as the rest, isn't it?'

'She said, 'Fire it!'' He repeated the words as if he actually heard her saying them again.

'And she was standing there looking at you?'

He did not answer.

'So you shot her in a blind rage and made a better shot than a Wild West film star!' I took another short drink. 'In a blind rage. Now let's see how rageful it was.

'She taunted you. You saw the gun,

58

went to the table, picked it up, looked for the catch, tried which way it went, freed it, then pointed the gun and fired. Boy! That's some blind rage. You must have been blind for several seconds.'

'I don't remember doing any of those things,' he said.

'But you must have done them!'

'Obviously.'

'Are you going to plead a breakdown? You have the history. It's the obvious defence.'

'I can't do that.'

'Why not? It's the truth, isn't it?'

'I shot her. I shall go through with it. I don't believe in wriggling out. No, I couldn't do that.'

'Don't let me have the boy scout angle. The fact is, never, in your normal life, would you have done this thing. That is the fact, isn't it?'

'Of course it is! You don't think — ' He cut off and just shrugged. 'But I did, you see.'

'Do you actually remember doing it?'

'No. I think I have told you before, I don't recall the details. But obviously, they did occur. The girl is dead and there was no third person here.'

'Then where is your brief-case?'

'Obviously, I must have been mistaken about bringing it. I am depending on what I am certain I would do. But the girl's death proved I can't be certain any more. I must have left the case downstairs.'

'You make me tired!' I said. 'You can't remember a damned thing yet you still swear you weren't ill. Why are you frightened to admit the illness?'

'I can't afford it,' he shouted back. 'Everything depends on handling the present — the situation. Everything.'

'The responsibility has got you down.'

'I can't let it!' He stamped up to the window and turned. 'I was quite normal when I arrived here.'

'All right, Lord Normal,' I said bitterly. 'You were dead ordinary this morning. Nothing wrong with you. Your mind clear, your nerves smooth as silk. I believe you. Provided you can answer one question.'

'What?'

'Where were you between half past nine and half past eleven this morning?'

*   *   *

He threw himself on to the settee at the window.

'I can't remember,' he said, and grunted. 'All right. Admitted. Amnesia. The time is lost, so there must be something wrong again.'

'Well, fill in up to half-nine,' I said.

'I was later than usual getting up. Tired.' He made a grimace. 'Yes, I admit I was tired from the start. I had breakfast down in the service restaurant.'

'Is that usual?'

'No. I was late. Also my woman who does and cooks breakfast doesn't come in on Saturdays. If I have no appointments, I cook for myself. If I have, I feed downstairs.'

'You took the brief-case down with you?'

'Yes. It is very important. That's why I cannot imagine myself leaving it somewhere when I got here.'

'Feeling that you were in the house of the ally, you might have relaxed your normal vigilance.'

'Could be. I don't know.'

'After breakfast the company car was waiting for you with the new driver?'

'Yes.'

'What kind of flats are these?'

'A block downriver. It overlooks the Thames. I have a penthouse.'

'With every mod. con?'

He shrugged. 'Hot water, hot air, hot food. Yes.'

'You got in the car and started work on your papers in the brief-case. You said that before. Do you remember exactly what work you did?'

'I was just checking details.'

'Do you remember them?'

'Not specifically. It was arranging things for the interview, getting the whole picture to be presented.'

'And it took you nearly two hours.'

'Heavens, no! Now could it?'

'Where else could you have been but in the car?'

'But my watch said quarter to ten

when I got here.'

'Check it now. Two-five.'

'About that,' he said.

'There's a time slip in your head or in that watch,' I said. 'You've lost ninety minutes somewhere.'

He made a helpless gesture with his hands.

'What's your daily woman like?'

'Mrs. Pleasance? Very good indeed. A widow.'

'What age?'

'Thirty-five. She's not quite the ordinary woman. She does various services for me, drives, is a bit of a secretary, too, when needed. All the hard cleaning is done by the flats staff.'

'You had a blackout,' I said.

He didn't say anything. He couldn't very well argue any more about it. I saw his face shining a bit and he wiped his forehead with a handkerchief. He was scared of the blackout.

'The point is where did you come out of it?'

'Downstairs when I got that lager in the bar. I don't really remember anything before that, except going through the papers.'

'And you're not so damn sure you remember anything up to the time I came in. Are you?'

I went close up and glared at him.

'You're not sure, are you?'

'It's hazy,' he said.

'Like it was before when you broke down?'

'Like that.'

'Do you feel you might have taken some drug this morning?'

He started.

'God, no! What made you say that?' He was scared again.

'An easy way to lose time out is to take drugs,' I said. 'In fact, it's probably the easiest.'

'But I had breakfast in the public restaurant. You're not suggesting the food could have been doped?'

'Forget it. It was just an idea.'

'Are you trying to work out that I didn't kill that girl?'

'I'm trying to work out what it's all about, one way or the other. It's interesting, and for Pete's sake, there's nothing else to do, is there?'

Instinctively we both stopped talking and listened. There was no sound in the place. Even the fridge was in between whispers.

'Let's leave you,' I said, 'and take me. Your secretary and I rang near the same time yesterday. My appointment is in Marsh's diary. Yours isn't. Is that significant?'

'You mean my call was intercepted and never got here?'

'That argues LOHM is innocent.' I watched the window for a moment as a car went by on the road.

'It would also seem to argue that my call was intercepted in my own offices. I can't see where else the tap could be made.'

'I take it you came to see Marsh because you were worried over some espionage in your own offices,' I said. 'So what's odd?'

He shrugged.

'As you say, it begins to clear things for LOHM, taken from one view.'

'Suppose they are clear,' I said. 'Where the hell are they?'

'Don't ask me. Get back to you. Who are you?'

So I told him a few details.

'There's a common factor,' he said. 'Money.'

'It would take a good belly dancer to skin me out of mine,' I said. 'I had a difficult time once and from then on I trust nobody, at least for the first five minutes.'

'But it is a factor.'

'It is. But what have I to do with this murder? I was led in because it would have been too anti-social to break into my flat and strap me to the bed to stop me coming. Besides, I am a witness against you.'

'Then why lock you in?'

'A good question. I don't know the answer unless it is just to keep me in cold storage until Monday, when we both get found.'

I thought of something then and went and lifted the bedspread.

'That's about a thirty-eight bust,' I

said, dropping it again.

'How do you know?' he said.

I went out without answering and pulled the drawers in the bedroom. There were several brassières there, and when I made sure I went back to Kilgallen.

'The girl lives here is thirty-four,' I said. 'So it's not this one on the floor.'

'You can't tell just by looking.'

'Thirty-four is small. You'll see that one is on the big side.'

'I accept the expert evidence.' He meant he didn't want to look at her again. 'So she doesn't live here.'

'She's a dud Sheila, perhaps. Doesn't belong to LOHM. Still perhaps. But where is the real one? Where are her three partners? I don't know Marsh's handwriting, but my name in that diary was the same hand as the other entries, so I assume he wrote it when he was told about the appointment.'

'Then he went away for a long weekend.'

'Or taken away for the same. But how do you kidnap four fully alert, anti-espionage experts in their own nest?

You'd have to do it all at once and in silence. Silence in case anyone else was about to hear a commotion. And according to my evidence, it must have happened three minutes before I got here. How did they get the four away without a sound and without me seeing any vehicle?'

'You saw none at all?'

'I saw a lawn mower and rider which I wish I'd taken a closer look at. But I didn't think anything was wrong then. All was so peaceful.'

'You then just walked into a trap?'

'No. I looked around, wondering what had gone wrong. That was a weak point if there are kidnappers. I might have got the wind that something was disastrously wrong and phoned the police. In fact, I did go back to the pub and tell the landlord the oddness of what I'd found. He was most interested, and I should think he won't keep quiet about it.'

'Except that I assume it's none of his business.'

'You would be right there. He won't act. Just talk.'

'But one would think you would have been trapped first, not afterwards.'

'Except for the fact that you were not here then. It was after I'd gone that they arranged the girl to be up here and brought you in.'

'I can't believe that.'

'Just ask me. I didn't miss a second of this fine day. I can account for the lot, and I have the landlord witness who spoke with me for some time. And another, now I come to think. The gardener was here. He, too, was surprised there was no LOHM about. He says there were always some of them around every Saturday.'

He got up.

'Isn't there some way out of this den? There must be one!'

'Smash the main door?' I said. 'Do you think it would be smashable, when everything else isn't?'

'We can try.'

'Okay. We'll try. With what?'

We looked through the flat. There was good furniture, very good, and nothing whatever suitable to bash doors in with.

Kilgallen took a rush at it and banged it with his shoulder. He nearly broke his collarbone. I didn't see the door shiver much.

'Bloody block of concrete,' he said, panting and holding his shoulder.

'I tried the windows with a hammer,' I said.

'Let us try again, scientifically,' he said.

We got the hammer and came back to the lounge, which had the biggest window.

'If we tap it rhythmically in the centre of the pane,' he said, 'we might start it springing. Then it will shatter itself.'

'I don't think you realise how thick it is,' I said. 'But it's worth the try.'

He tried, tapping rhythmically, almost musically, and the echoes from the glass certainly began to take on a different tone after a half-minute, which showed at least that it was vibrating.

He had a good idea there, and it would certainly have worked, if we had known what the frequency of the glass was. It was the old Caruso trick of smashing the wine-glass with resonance, but this was half-inch plate and its resonance period would have been too far out even for Caruso.

He tired suddenly and threw the hammer across the room.

Just for the joke, we tried the phones again. If there had been just one mocking laugh at the other end it would have been something. There wasn't anything at all. The line wasn't even live.

'There must be a way out!' he shouted. 'We can't just be cut off like this in the middle of a civilised country!'

That he should have kept bursting into such banalities showed how far gone he was from what must have been his usual sharply intelligent outlook. By that time I had the idea, unspoken then, that someone was deliberately playing on his fears for his mental stability.

If that was true, then he was going all out to help them. Perhaps he couldn't help that, either.

The items were heavily stacked against him. The photographs he had never been in and showed him there; the girl he had murdered whom he had never seen; the

71

time shift which lost ninety minutes somewhere. Things like that were enough to shake even a firmly balanced, unimaginative mind. Stacked against a man frightened of a return to a breakdown, they were terrifying.

The fact of being shut in and unable to get out, perhaps for days, added to the gathering of fear all round him.

'You said you'd had difficult times before,' he said suddenly. 'Do you mean hard up?'

'Never that. Involvement with criminal types. My fault. I just didn't realise where I was heading.'

'Could all this be anything to do with people you once got involved with?' he asked, suddenly eager. 'It might explain a lot.'

'I have tried to think along those lines, but I can't think of anyone who would take a hand in industrial spying.'

'It's a widening business all the time,' he said. 'It pays very large sums, and unless you're very unlucky, the risk isn't great.'

'Of the people I have called to mind,' I

said, 'some are dead and the rest in jug. Take it from there. If there is some connection to my earlier affairs, it could be that I am wanted as a witness. I can't think of anything else.'

'They want to finish me. That's clear. They've done it, too. If only I hadn't seen red like that!'

'It was a pretty risky plot if it depended on you seeing red at a given moment when the girl was in front of you and the gun hard by. The odds against everything happening as they wanted are millions to one.'

'But it happened,' he said.

'That's the interesting part. Not the murder, but that the plot worked just as if you were a puppet on strings. How did they know that you would jerk the way they wanted?'

'They knew about the mental illness.'

'But you were never violent?'

'No. But you can never be sure.'

There seemed no point in arguing on that. I went out into the hall again and looked at the door, as if I might have overlooked some easy way by which it could be opened without the key.

And while I stood there I heard the soft click of a key being put into the lock on the outside.

4

There wasn't much time between the quiet click of the key and the moment the door began to open. I got to one side of it and as soon as an arm appeared in the gap I grabbed it and pulled the owner in head-long.

There was a squeak, or part of a scream, or just a bursting noise of surprise as the person went past me, clutching out at me to save herself.

For it was a girl, but there was no time to see what kind before the door slammed shut and the key clicked again. It was done so quickly there was just no time to get a foot in the opening after the girl had gone by.

'Done it again!' I said, and tried to grab the door open.

But it was really only temper and frustration that made me try it. I knew it wouldn't open.

The girl recovered very quickly and

turned, a tall, irate, fashionably thin girl; the blonde model on the magazine covers. She glared so that her blue eyes seemed lit up.

'What the merry hell — ' she began.

'Be calm,' I interrupted.

'Calm? Who are you? Who shut that door? What's this on my floor — ?'

She saw what it was because the bedspread clung fairly well to the figure of the dead girl.

'Good God!' she said. 'What kind of drama's this?'

She bent and snatched up a corner of the sheet. She stayed a moment looking, then let it down very gently.

She looked at me. She looked at Kilgallen.

'Somebody better tell,' she said, and put her handbag on a hall table. 'Who are you? What's happened?'

'You said *your* floor,' I said. 'Is this your flat?'

'I wouldn't have the key to anybody else's,' she snapped.

'You haven't got one to this flat now,' I said, 'Unless you have a spare?'

'I don't carry two,' she said, and looked down at the heap again. 'Who's that under there?'

'Look, are you a partner in LOHM? Sheila whatever it is?'

'Sheila, yes. But who are the rest of us?'

She didn't wait for an answer but walked off quickly through the flat, long-legged, swinging, attractively angry. She came back smoking a new cigarette.

'Where's everybody downstairs? What's happening?' she demanded, glaring from Kilgallen to me.

I told her in very few words the bald details of how I had come in, been trapped and found K and the dead girl.

'She said she was Sheila?' the girl said. 'Well, she could have been. I don't like the coincidence. Too grotty. A blackmail set-up.' She frowned and for a moment looked lost. 'In my flat! Grottier and grottier! But where's John, Mary, Jane? There's not a soul downstairs. And who locked that bloody door?'

She went out in a rage and pushed and pulled it. Then she came back and went to the phone. I think she had tried one in the bedroom because she didn't look as if she expected any change out of the experiment.

In spite of an apparent air of smartness and *savoir faire* she was quite clearly confused. She was doing things in the wrong order, and I thought it would be best to leave her to come off the simmer before getting any real information out of her.

'Lord Kilgallen,' she said, cooling a bit. 'Jonathan Blake. I've heard of both of you. But what are you doing here in my flat? It's all so odd it seems like a dream. And a murder. That's no dream. I've got over feeling sick. This is going to be a bad thing for the firm. I can't think what in hell's happened to them!'

'We worked it that possibly Kilgallen's call didn't get here, but we have written proof that mine did,' I said. 'Now John Marsh doesn't sound like a man who'd make a date then walk out on it two minutes before it was due.'

'He wouldn't,' she said. 'We're here in business, not amateur dramatics. But what did happen to him? And the girls?'

'Well, what happened to you?' I said. 'Let's start with that.'

'Nothing happened to me. I had a date for Friday night, last night, and it went on late so I stayed in town by arrangement with a girl-friend.'

'You arranged that beforehand?'

'Yes. In this outfit everybody must know where everybody else is — unless they're on holiday. We are a very small band and the maximum use has to be made of everybody's position on the board — that is, the games board.'

'Are you back on time?'

'I am. In fact a half hour early. This is a dead mystery! I can't think what's happened!'

'Let's get rid of you first,' I said. 'This date. Was it your making?'

'No. I was invited.'

'On the firm's behalf?'

'No. A boy from an agency. Ad man. We had dinner, saw a show, then had supper at a club. What's the good of keeping your figure too sharp? The old crossed knitting needle shape will be out soon.'

'What agency?'

'Calif-Brent.'

Kilgallen broke in.

'They tried to make our account,' he said. 'But we have been tied up with Matheson for a long time. They handle the account well. No reason for change.'

'Do you model for Calif?' I said.

'No. I freelance among the photographers, though not much now I put my grist into this mill.' She sat down suddenly in a chair. She was knocked.

'Do you know this girl here?' I said. 'We don't.'

'I've seen her round the studios,' Sheila said. 'I'm sure her name is Bet Wain. Mostly nudes, as I remember. Poses for camera clubs altogether. I think that's it.'

She got up and went over and after a slight hesitation, had another look. She nodded, then straightened.

'Poor kid,' she said, with a flicker of anger. 'Why did you do a thing like that? A man like you?'

Kilgallen just didn't answer. I could see his jaw muscles working, as if his jaw was too taut to let him speak.

'There are several things we don't understand about all this,' I said. I told her a few, about the slow motion actions with the gun, seeing it, taking it up, snapping the unknown catch, firing just one shot from seven.

'He must have done his nut,' She said, and stared at Kilgallen's back. 'Even with a lot at stake, why murder? It makes everything worse.'

'We can't do much about that section of the puzzle,' I said, 'because he says he did it, though he can't remember any details. What interests me most is what happened to the ninety minutes.'

I gave it to her clearly again so she could get the action foot by foot.

'Blackout,' she said. 'What else?'

'But what about the convenience of the coincidence?' I said. 'A blackout just when it suits the plot. Surely that smells grotty to you?'

Kilgallen turned to watch me.

'You're on with this drug again,' he said. 'I tell you I have had experience of such drugs under treatment, and there has been nothing today which signals any sort of drug effects I have known. Besides, how could it have been given? I ate in a public restaurant, travelled in my own car, smoked my own cigarettes. I was not scratched or pushed or needled. I did not smell anything, nor inhale anything but ordinary tobacco smoke.'

He insisted. He kept on insisting. He even insisted he had shot her, though we had never found his briefcase. I still had the idea that the missing case could have proved a third person was in the flat at the time of the shooting or round about it.

But to keep going on over the same ground was tracking in a lost circle in a desert.

I thought I heard something outside and tried the flat door again. It was still locked solid.

'Do you know if your partners had any appointments today apart from mine?' I asked her.

'This looks a bit of a stinker as far as we're concerned,' she said. 'Lord Kilgallen thinks this set-up is meant to ruin him, but it will surely ruin us, too. Who will trust us after this?'

The double knock did not interest me then, because I was not sure about LOHM anyhow. A firm dealing in other firms' secrets is in a better position for blackmail or pressure than anyone coming in from outside.

There was also a link between the two girl models.

'Do you know what they meant to do today?'

'There's no fitness classes, Saturday or Sunday,' she said. 'Fencing, judo, shooting, what have you, are all by appointment at weekends, but the week-ends don't bring in a lot. Most customers would sooner spend firms' time during the week than their own at weekends.'

'Do you know if there are any appointments?'

'As I remember, no. I don't think there were any.' She looked a bit puzzled. 'Is that unusual?'

'Very. There's usually something going on, actively. Not a lot, but always something. I don't remember a weekend that was dead empty, come to think.'

She walked to the window and looked out at the empty garden. Then she turned round.

'Look here! We can't stay shut up like this!'

'But surely the others might come back?'

'Might come back? They should be here now! There's always one of us here. It's a rule.'

'Then what's broken it?'

'You came and found a stationary *Marie Celeste*. Well, it never happened in my time. The coffee, the cigarette — It almost seems somebody saw you coming and cleared everybody out.'

'Exactly. How?'

'At the gun point. What other way is there to make people troop out of their own place?'

'Sounds too easy. There were three, all used to a little roughish stuff on occasion. Do you mean all three were taken completely by surprise, were silenced and carted off without any noise or upset at all? Even the commandos had to make some noise, even if only in breaking a neck.'

'Gas,' she said. 'That was used here before, I remember. They shoved it in through the air conditioner.'

'But it wouldn't have cleared in three minutes,' I said. 'I'd have had some.'

'Yes. That won't work.'

'Further, I was let in, and so were you and nothing was done to us in the way of violence. We were just locked in here. In my case I could have raised a police scream while I was at the pub. They didn't know I wouldn't.'

'So you really think it's us all the time?' she said, with a small, twisted smile.

'What else? How do three people melt away unless by their own wish?'

'And what can we gain by stuffing our business down a drain?' she asked, scornfully.

'You might be entering on another form of business,' I said.

'I suppose we're all crooks at heart,' she said, turning away angrily, 'but I can't say I like being called one!'

'One gets used to it,' I said. 'Just tell me

what everything was like downstairs when you came in.'

'Just plain dead,' she said, and shrugged. 'But the lager glass you saw, the coffee and all that had gone. I didn't see any of them.'

'And the diary was open on the desk?'

'There wasn't anything on the desk but the phones and the intercom, and an ash-tray. A clean ash-tray.'

'The mail was on the little table in the other office.'

'Yes. That was there. I looked through. None of it seemed important. We get days like that.'

'What about the letter from Perpignan?'

She frowned at me.

'There was no letter from Perpignan,' she said. 'There was no foreign mail at all.'

'Have we got a clue?' I said.

★　★　★

'I've got a house there,' Kilgallen said. It was the first time he had spoken for a long while. 'I haven't used it for years. It was to be our retreat, but we didn't retreat together.'

'What happens to it?' I said.

'It's rented. Some sentiment makes me hang on to it. Furnished rental. Several families during the summer, and the agents usually find someone to take it through the winter. I ought to get rid of it.'

'When did you last go there?'

'Five years back, I should think.'

'What has LOHM to do with Perpignan?' I said to the girl.

'LOHM has to do with anywhere,' she said. 'Clients pop up all over. I think Perpignan was something to do with a fencing job. Foils, that is, not putting a fence round.'

'Do you know who it was?'

'A French industrialist. I think it's aircraft. I'm not sure of that. Jane was dealing with it. The notes are downstairs.'

'He was coming for fencing practice, or tuition, or what?'

'Tuition or what, both,' she said. 'They don't usually come a long way just for sport. There's usually some other reason. Our business is undercover, as you know already, so that before we've met a client we don't know anything but who he is, where he comes from, what his social rating is. We don't know the truth until he spills it. Sometimes he doesn't. Sometimes the trouble gets cleared before we're consulted.'

'What's his name?' Kilgallen said, coming out of a dream. 'Henri Marc?'

'Indeed it is.' She showed a slight surprise, but it soon faded. 'But then all you tycoons know each other.'

'I don't know him,' Kilgallen said. 'I rented him my house for three months. It was just the coincidence.'

'All these coincidences,' I said, 'Grotty increases.'

'You can make coincidences,' Kilgallen said, 'by looking at effects and ignoring causes.'

'You wouldn't know this Marc if you saw him?' I asked.

'That applies to everyone I've dealt with since I got here,' he said, and shrugged. 'The thing that interests me, madam, is what chances there are your partners will turn up today?'

'I don't even know why they're not here now,' she said. 'They said the locks here are almost unpickable.'

'I should say it doesn't matter,' I said. 'We've got no instruments. We've tried most things to get out. Unless you can remember something we didn't think of.'

'The key to the back door's gone,' she said. 'It always hangs on a hook behind the fridge. Someone knew. They took it.'

'Would you say that whoever's messing around knows this place well?' I said.

'Yes. I should say they did. At least, to know about that key.'

'What about the ad man you went to dinner with last night? Has he been up here?'

'Look, Jimmy Consol is a friend of mine!' She flared up.

'Then he's one we can rule out,' I said. 'Although he is another coincidence, isn't he?'

She turned her back.

'I'll get a snack together,' she said. 'I'm starving.'

She went out.

'Why doesn't something happen?' Kilgallen snapped when we were alone.

'Don't worry. It will,' I said. 'I can feel it.'

We stayed still, listening for the hundredth time. Beyond the faint noise of the girl in the kitchen, there wasn't a sound in the world.

'What makes you think so?' he said.

'The girl coming back. If somebody outside has fixed all this, they've collared the other three. Surely they should have collared the fourth?'

'In view of the fact she might be able to help us?'

'She might have had another key. How did they know she hadn't?'

'Mr. Consol, who knows all about keys,' said Kilgellan, dryly. 'I'm too bloody depressed to bother. After all these hours, it's only now that I'm beginning to realise I'm done for. Some things are such a shock they don't seem real. This one's just getting real. It's burning black.'

'Don't let go,' I said. 'It's too early.'

'Are you off your head, man?' he cried.

'What chance is there to get out of the mess I'm in?'

'I've been in a lot of messes,' I said. 'Sometimes I've felt like you, but then I'm an up-and-downer, like you. I'm either bouncing with misplaced confidence or dead sure I'll die. But when I think it's usually on the mean average line between the two, and that helps. You might get away with this.'

'Guilty but insane?' he said bitterly. 'That would be a charming way out, wouldn't it?'

'Suppose we could show there was a third person in this flat at the time of the murder?' I said.

'Supposing!' He laughed. 'But I saw nobody but the girl!'

'You don't even remember what happened, so how can you be sure of one thing and not of another?'

'Hair splitting,' he said savagely. 'There will have to be a trial, won't there? What's the evidence, then? Those photographs. The public mind, when it gets a taint from things like that, is made up against you at the start. You can't break it down.

It's latent Puritanism. It'll beat all the Catholics.'

'There is still a chance,' I said, getting angry myself at his determination to sink.

'What does it matter? You can't keep anything quiet in this day and age. How are you going to prove some third person was here? And if you do, how will you prove the pictures were faked?'

'Difficult questions,' I said. 'I'm not a detective. I've just got a criminal mind. Thief to catch thief. I've been trying to put myself in the position of doing this to do to benefit myself. Do you know, I wouldn't do one single thing that's been done up to now.'

'Why not?'

'Because each move depends on the staggering luck of you doing exactly what you are planned to do. That wouldn't work for me.'

He walked to the window and back.

'There must be something backstage you can't see,' he said. 'That's the reason for the risk. Perhaps it isn't such a risk as it appears.'

'Obviously there must be something,' I said. 'And it's looking for that I'll be. The puzzle is that you met it and I didn't. And no matter how often I go back on what we both did, I can't just see where this invisible thing came in.'

'You're not suggesting someone invisible?' he looked incredulous.

'Heavens, no! Get with it! I once came across some invisibility but it was done with subliminal pictures. Flicking one in your sight on top of what you should really be seeing. It works. It needs stamping out. I'm sure this is none of that.'

Then suddenly it happened. It split the quiet afternoon like a great strike slitting everything apart.

The telephone rang.

He was quicker than I, for he had been standing right by it. He snatched it up and barked into it.

Then he stopped still. I watched him. If anyone was speaking at the other end they must have been whispering, for I heard no familiar cackle from the earpiece he held against his head.

The odd quiet went on. He was staring at the wall.

'Is there anyone there?' I asked suddenly.

He slammed the phone down. Very slowly he turned towards me. He didn't say anything, but I could see something had happened — snapped perhaps.

He made a sudden dive for the gun lying in my handkerchief on the table. He got there a part second before I did and had a hold on it when I got his wrist.

There was an off balance struggle for a moment, he straining to turn the gun on me, and me trying to break his wrist before he could. But neither of us had proper balance and our actions were weak.

He staggered forward, and I tried to pull him, but hadn't the foot grip for it. We reeled about together for a moment, and then I got a full grip on his gun wrist and forced it down.

He pulled the trigger. The gun blasted its guts into the carpet to the last shot. Then he dropped the gun and started fighting with his fist and knees and everything else, including his head.

I was butted in the middle so hard I went backwards to the sofa, and as I landed I saw him pouncing on me in a mad rage.

My gymnastic practice is sometimes useful. I used the momentum of my backward fall to swing my legs up and do a turn over the back of the sofa, landing on my feet.

Frustrated, he picked up the table and slung it at me. I ducked that and it crashed against the wall, bringing down a mirror with a shattering tinkling.

He ran round the end of the sofa. He looked like a wild bull man. I have faced a few murderous men in fights, but never one I felt so suddenly shocked by as Kilgallen.

He was staring, raving mad, and he was going to get me no matter what stood in the way.

Fighting a sane man is one thing. He thinks sanely and you can counteract him because automatically, he follows certain rules.

Kilgallen had never fought, I should

say. He just had size, strength and a murderous instinct to smash whatever stood in his way.

I countered his wild arms but couldn't stop his kick nearly splitting my thigh. I managed to clump him on the side of his face and knocked him against the wall, his feet grinding away on the shattered glass.

'What's the matter? Stop it! Stop it!'

I heard Sheila crying out from the open doorway, but Kilgallen paid no attention to her. He recovered his balance and came again.

This time I got a grip and swung him clean over the sofa. He thumped on to the carpet, but rolled over and was up quicker than an ape, ready to meet me as I ran round.

The girl came to grab him. He just put a huge hand in her chest and shoved her back so that she thumped into an arm-chair with her head flopping like a doll's.

He came for me again, swiping now, in some semblance of boxing. I sliced a couple of those blows away, but they were too hard and heavy to be parried. He broke through with one and nearly knocked my head off.

I was dazed by it, and the instinct to save myself was the only thing that kept me on my feet. I went back against the wall.

Through the haze I saw him snatch up a chair and raise it above his head with both hands.

All I could do was just roll along the wall, and the chair crashed into splinters and a falling seat against the plaster.

While he still had bits of it in his big hands, I got him on the side of the face with a hard left. He shook his head, but he reeled sideways under it, and I went to go in again.

He had a foot long piece of the chair back in his hand, the splintered end like a dagger. He raised it as such and stabbed at me as hard as he could.

It ripped the shoulder of my jacket right through and I felt the burn of my skin tearing.

I got him in the belly with a right, then grabbed the arm which had rammed past my shoulder. I got it good this time, and used his own forward movement to send him on his way.

He went headlong. I thought he would go through the big window in his wild effort to keep on his feet by running.

He hit the arm of the settee there, spun round and rocked.

'Get him now!' the girl shouted.

She was on my right, running in. She got his left arm in a lock. He twisted to crash his right fist down on her head it seemed, but he hadn't time.

I clocked him. I made no mistake about it this time. It had to be one-out, and after that, find out what the hell had happened.

It seemed for a moment after the blow connected that he wouldn't drop after all. He just stood there rocking slowly, the girl clinging to his left arm. Then his knees gave, very slowly, and he went down almost peacefully.

She let go. He went face forward to the carpet and laid there, out.

'Good lord! What happened?' she panted.

'He answered the phone and then went

off his head. Did you answer from the other room?'

'No. I heard him shout out hallo. Then I didn't hear anything. The damn kettle started to boil. I went back and switched it off. I thought it funny nobody was speaking. I went into the bedroom and lifted the phone there. It was dead, as before.'

'Dead?'

She nodded.

'So somebody rang and then killed it again after he rang off. Or was it after?'

'Just as I found it dead, I heard the shots.'

'That fixes the time.'

I looked at him lying there, breathing hard. There was the answer to the mystery, in that big, pulsing head. But I don't think he even knew it.

'Well, it fixes one thing,' she said, going to the cigarette box. 'He's mad as a bull. He could easily have shot that girl as he tried to shoot you.'

5

The girl said, 'Take your jacket off. I'll get the first-aid.'

I got it off. There was blood over my shirt, and the shoulder of it had been ripped in a tear six inches across.

Kilgallen lay flat on the floor breathing like a fallen ox. I think his pressurised state of nerves must have helped to keep him out so long by sheer reaction. He looked almost glad to be out and not know what was going on.

She came back. She was good and quick at the dressing, which showed she had had training.

'You notice,' she said, 'I didn't use any judo throws on him. Had it been Jane she would have thrown him through the window. My job in the public eye is running the bar and catering. I think you near killed him.'

'He's resting,' I said. 'He's had a rough time.'

'Why in hell did he go for you like that?'

'He went off his onion — flip! Like that.'

'Something on the phone sent him?'

'I didn't hear anybody on the phone.'

'Well, how long did he stand there listening?'

'Thirty seconds, I'd say.'

'Long time for nobody there.'

'He looked half-daft. Almost paralysed. Something happened to him, but I didn't hear anything happening on the phone. Put it like that.'

'You mean he really is a nut case?'

'I don't see how he can be. A man in his position, which he's reached on his own brain, can't be a raving lunatic at the turn of a page. There's something wrong. I think he was doped somehow, in spite of what he says.'

Kilgallen started to come to. She was mopping his face with cold water then, but for a minute or so it hadn't seemed to help. Like her, I had begun to feel uneasy about the length of his stay in dreamland.

She sat back on her haunches and he

101

clambered into a sitting position and shook his big head.

He mumbled but I didn't make out any words. He looked round him, then realised he was sitting on the floor, rolled over and got up. He dusted himself down and stared at me, then at the girl.

He didn't have to say anything about what he felt. We could see from his expression that he was wondering where the hell he was.

'Remember me?' I said. 'You just ripped a square foot of skin off my shoulder.'

'I remember you,' he said, frowning. 'Of course. But what happened to me? A blackout! Hell! I knew it!'

But he felt his jaw suddenly and touched it, and then he stared harder.

'I knocked you out,' I said. 'Case of have to. You needn't worry about blackout. It was externally induced.'

He sat down, slowly, watching me, trying hard to remember.

'Remember the phone call?' I said.

He looked round then.

'I thought the phones were dead!' he

said, and reached out.

'They are. But they rang once, just now. And you answered.'

He dropped his hand and then shook his head. Sheila got up from the floor, gathered up the first-aid things. I picked up the basin of water for her and we went out by the door through the bedroom. Nobody wanted to go near the other doorway.

'You'd better eat something,' she called back over her shoulder. 'You'll feel better.'

He followed us, shambling along like a big ape, dragging, nearly. His depression could almost be seen over his head in a black cloud, as in a comic strip.

I thought that if his persecution went on much longer he would certainly be back in the mind bin.

We had tea in the kitchen and ate cucumber sandwiches. At least, the girl and I did. Kilgallen drank tea and scowled out of the windows all the time.

'We must try and get out of this place,' I said. 'Can you think of any way that we haven't considered yet? With no tools all the obvious ways are barred. Is there a ventilating shaft one could wriggle through? A service lift I didn't notice?'

'That's one of the vents up there,' she said, pointing. 'I reckon half of you could wriggle through, but I haven't an axe to get rid of the unwanted half.'

'Where are the tanks?' I said, suddenly remembering this necessary item. 'The water tanks?'

'On the roof, I suppose,' she said. 'They would have to be above, wouldn't they?'

'Yes, but when I came I didn't notice if there was a tank house on the flat roof or not. Is there?'

'What's it look like?'

'A brick box stuck on top of the building. There should be one for the lift works also. I noticed a lift downstairs.'

'No,' she said. 'The roof's flat. Absolutely.'

'Then the tanks and the lift works must be in an attic between this ceiling and the roof above. Let's look for a trap in the ceiling somewhere.'

We started a search of the flat. The architect had decided to hide all sordid details like traps in the ceiling, and in the end we came to the bedroom.

The ceiling there was broken into squares. I got a chair and started pushing up each square until I found one that gave way and showed a black hole above.

'I never knew that,' said Sheila.

'By God, it's a way out!' Kilgallen shouted. 'At last!'

I couldn't get close enough to haul up with only the chair height, and my shoulder had gone solid, which didn't help. We pushed the dressing table over and from the glass top I got a height enough to let me pull up through the hole.

When I got through and stood up I found it wasn't entirely dark. Some daylight was filtering through air bricks round the walls, and these patterned light spots showed the considerable extent of the attic.

I could see the sides of the tank cases and the lift motor and gears were almost in the middle of the big room.

It was a very odd piece of design altogether, with the flat roof supported on concrete pillars. But it occurred to me that this might be intended for some future development, which justified its cost.

Clearly there would be trapdoors to each flat on the floor below. But I felt sure that by now the outer doors of those flats would all be locked, so that even if I got inside they would stay locked, for want of keys.

It would be getting myself out of a small prison into a larger one. But still, some chance might offer itself.

So I went round in the gloom and looked for other trapdoors which from the top, would be easy to see.

I found the first one beyond the tanks. I bent and got a good hold of the lifting ring. I pulled, and the ring pulled back. The trap didn't move. It was locked below.

That was a shock. I found the other two and they also were locked below.

I looked round the silent place, and the only living thing there was me. At this point it seemed necessary to think things out as a protection against doing my nut from sheer frustration.

It looked as if I had been intended to get up here. If it hadn't the trap I had come through could have been fixed from above.

'Have you found anything?'

Kilgallen's voice echoed in the place. I went back to the trap and looked down into his upturned face.

'There isn't a way out of here that I can see,' I said. 'But I'll go on looking. You stay down there in case.'

'I can't get myself up through the trap, anyway,' he said. 'Out of condition.'

'I shouldn't have thought so,' I said. 'Hang on, anyhow. I'll yell if there's anything.'

The first thing I could think of was to go round all the walls and see if there was an outside opening in them. There would have to be something of the sort for bringing in new tanks, lift motors or machinery that might go wrong up there.

There was such an opening, held fast by a thick oak door, held shut by three hefty bolts.

They all slid back easily, and my spirits

began to bubble up as I gripped the iron handle and pulled the heavy door. It didn't give, so I pushed and it did. It swung out and I nearly went with it.

The ground below looked a couple of miles down, and I got hold of the door jamb just in time. This was just a service door that opened into the pure open air. There were no steps, no ladders, no nothing. The roof parapet was too high above me to get a hold on. There was nothing but brick to the sides and below.

Before me, fields spread out running away into woods in the distance. The opening faced away from the road. I left the door open and went back to the attic to have a closer look around with the added light from the doorway.

By then I was expecting to find something, but I didn't know what. The whole thing, till then, had been a lunatic rigmarole that seemed to have no other purpose than to wreck Kilgallen career-wise and mentally. Almost, it seemed, to make sure that nothing worth looking at was left of him.

That the plot had also got rid of a girl

that the operators didn't want could be coincidental, fortuitous or a pleasant side profit.

But I just couldn't get the angle as to why I had been jumped in with K., or why the girl had been let come back and into her own flat.

First, I might have said anything down at the pub. I might even have alerted the police. They didn't know I hadn't any good reason for doing such a thing. They had run a surprising risk considering what they proposed to do.

Second, Sheila had come back and after a brief look at the mail down there, and a glance into the empty offices, had come upstairs to freshen up.

She could have smelt something on down there and not come upstairs at all.

There was a point: they had cleared up the things which I had seen lying around, so that when Sheila saw the offices they just looked as if the cleaners had left and nobody had come in since. She had wondered where everybody was, yet still had come on up the stairs to her flat.

There, somebody had been waiting to lock her in.

She hadn't seen anyone, but the vestibule outside the flats had a couple of big chesterfields and some other furniture standing around. Hiding places enough for a few seconds' cover.

There was suddenly a hell of a clack behind me, and then the lift motor and gears started whining. For a moment I didn't know what it was. When I did I ran for it and tried to see if there was a spyhole slot where the cables ran down.

But without getting my head ground in the gears, it was impossible to see down.

The machinery stopped. It was maddening to know that someone was below and I couldn't see who. The silence fell again.

Then from nearby there was a hiss. That, too, puzzled me until I realised that someone was drawing off water below.

Back at the open trap I saw Kilgallen still down there. He jerked his face up as he heard me.

'Anybody running water down there?' I said.

He looked round him. Then I saw the girl was there, also looking up.

'No,' she said.

'Somebody must have got into one of the other flats. The lift just worked. Try the phone again.'

She did, but there was no dice. I told them the situation.

'Can we make a rope to get down from the door up there?' Kilgallen said, something of his boyhood returning to brighten his heavy face.

'It's a hell of a way down,' I said. 'But no harm in trying, if you've got enough sheets.'

'Just those on the bed,' Sheila said. 'We have a central linen store off the landing. The cleaners do all that.'

'Well, that isn't enough,' I said. 'With two sheets you'd break a leg. This door happens to be dead over a sunk concrete chute which, I assume, goes down to the boilers. Bad landing area.'

'Whenever there seems a way,' Kilgallen said, 'somebody has thought of it before.'

'Somebody knew about the linen being

all outside the flat,' I said. 'The finger's pointing to LOHM again.'

'You don't think I really want to be here. do you?' Sheila cried out 'Shut up here with a couple of murderous lunatics? For God's sake — '

'Cut it out. You're hysterical,' I shouted down at her.

That stopped her dead. She glared, but she didn't go on.

'Haven't you found anything up there?' she said, changing quickly. 'Anything besides the door?'

'I'm still trying,' I said, and went back to my search of the walls.

I hadn't much faith in finding anything useful.

★ ★ ★

One can be wrong because of knowledge which doesn't seem to apply. Early man must have seen metal glinting in ore but could not see a spear as a result. Finally, somebody did. I was, at the time, the goon who didn't.

The place seemed larger, darker, more

hopeless than ever. I carried on with the systematic search of the walls because I couldn't think of anything else.

I got nothing more from that — if you could count the door as anything useful to start with. I could have stood at it and bawled myself hoarse in the hope somebody might hear, but the most good that was likely to do was release some of my tensions. I didn't want to release any. I wanted to get some more and then come face to face with whoever was making monkeys of us.

I sat on one of the lift motor beams for a while, thinking it out again.

One thing which hadn't occurred was that Kilgallen had a vast list of employees, any dozen of which could hate his guts for reasons real or imagined. Bosses, as a class, are not generally liked.

He thought the call he made originally had been tapped in his own office — at least, he didn't protest too much about that idea. He had suggested it himself.

But he hadn't suggested any special person. That seemed a bit odd, because if he was ready to suspect he must have an idea where the suspicion came from, or who gave it to him.

Then I realised it wasn't much good using Kilgallen's talk as anything to go on. Whether drugs or instability returning or what, he couldn't remember some parts of what had happened to him. He just thought he did.

Thought he did.

Did he, then, remember *anything* he'd done that morning? Remember correctly, that is? If he didn't, then the loss of the ninety minutes was no longer a puzzle.

He just didn't know where in hell he was at. He kept saying he did to convince himself he was still all right in the head. Convince himself, not me.

But if I had to discard his witness altogether, what was left?

It left Sheila and myself as witnesses, and we hadn't seen anything happen except the door closing when I'd pulled her in.

Then I realised we hadn't even seen that. She had been coming in head-first, and I had been concentrating on doing it. My object had been to get the visitor in, not to stop anybody shutting the door.

I hadn't thought about anybody but the one person opening it.

Remembering that incident I recalled having had a faint uneasiness at seeing my visitor was a woman. I also remembered a feeling of alarm at thinking she would go straight on and smack her head against the wall. I don't like to knock walls with women's heads. It's a sign I'm still really frightened of my mother.

I tried to remember if I'd heard anything from beyond the opening, and that led me on to one thing which might have some meaning.

Whoever shut that door must have reached in.

Now if an arm had come in just at the moment I was pulling the girl past me, I would have caught it with the tail of my eye at the very least.

Shutting my eyes I saw the scene again like a replay from a film. I saw her hand appear, pushing the door open, then her jerking forward past me as I hauled her in. She had run on, but while she had done it, the door had slammed.

No arm had pulled it. I was sure of that, as I recalled every detail of that precipitate entry. I should have seen a hand, no matter what, because she had been past me by then and there had been nothing between me and the half-open door.

Then how in the world had the door been shut?

I noticed something was wrong but did not for a moment see what it was. Then I realised that slowly, the light was getting less. I turned to look across the wide space, but at that instant, the oak door closed firmly.

It seemed best for the moment to sit still and get used to the light pinpoints from the airbricks. After a moment the loss of the major source of light did not matter so much.

Backing away from the lift machinery I kept watching the gloom across the space where someone must be if he had closed that door.

Or was it another self-closing mechanism?

The thought that breeze might have

swung it I rejected for I remembered there had been practically none and I should have heard a sudden rising enough to slam the heavy door. Besides it had gone to quite slowly, not slammed.

Once more there came a hissing which grew prolonged and then grew louder. It sounded as if someone below had chosen this moment to take a bath, which was inconvenient, for it prevented me hearing anything of someone moving in the place.

At one moment I thought I saw a shadow flicker across one of the airbricks. I was not sure about it, but I made for the wall ahead of where I thought the shadow had been moving.

At the wall I stopped and looked along it. Even in that dim light I could see no one was there.

Running quickly the other way seemed a good idea, but I found no one there, either.

So I went back to the door and opened it again.

It stayed a moment, then began to close. I shoved against it and it stayed still, began to open again. Then it opened altogether.

Keeping to the side of the opening I squinted up to the parapet above me. I saw a rope with some kind of knob on the end snaking up. When the knob hit the coping there was a heavy thud and then the whole apparatus vanished.

A weight suspended from the roof, just dragging against the door and making it shut. The shadow I had seen crossing the airbrick had been the rope swinging.

A simple long distance trick. But how had that been worked in the flat where the door had to be *pulled* shut?

I went back to the trapdoor and got down to the dressing table, then to the floor.

'Well, what?' the girl said.

'Somebody on the roof,' I said. 'But you can't get at it. Where's Kilgallen?'

'Where he usually is — staring out of a window,' she said.

He was in the lounge staring out, his back to the girl's body.

'I heard you,' he said, without looking round. 'Somebody on the roof, somebody in the next flat. The place is getting crowded. Is it possible to get on the roof?'

'Given a grappling iron and a rope, yes. Without, no. One would also need artillery cover because whoever's on top might cut the ruddy rope.'

'We just don't move, do we?'

'You're always staring out of the window,' I said. 'Haven't you seen anyone out there?'

'Nobody,' he said. 'Perhaps they came by the back.'

I sat down and had a cigarette.

'Tell me about this house in Perpignan,' I said. 'Did you ever live in it?'

'I spent a little time there,' he said. 'A matter of weeks. Not all the time. I went because of business in Toulon. Combined the two, and also to decide what to do with the house.'

'Did your wife ever stay there?'

'Yes. She did. She stayed for a while after we parted.'

'I thought she ran away with somebody?'

'Not at first. She went to Perpignan to think things over. At the end of that time, she had decided against me.'

He looked grim and sad.

'I'm sorry to ask all this.'

'It's a long time ago,' he said gruffly.

'It could be important. Might give us a line,' I said. 'Who was the man?'

He looked grimmer.

'The man was a cheap bastard,' he said, almost snarling. 'That's not just jealousy. He wasn't worth a look from her. He was just one of those Romeos who hang around and hang around when they know a woman is getting lonely.'

'But he has stuck with her?'

'I give her a good income,' he said bitterly. 'She can support him.'

'He's that sort? But hasn't he a job?'

'He plays around at being a business consultant. He gets assignments, but he soon loses them. His main idea is to get his expensive tastes paid for, and firms get tired very quickly when results are a long time coming.'

'He has got connections, then?'

Kilgallen shrugged.

'He's doing his best to run out of them.'

'Has he ever done anything for you?'

'He has pestered me frequently. An organisation like ours has all the advisers it needs.'

I turned away from him then. Sheila was somewhere outside. I found her in the kitchen. She offered me more tea.

'It's fresh.'

'Yes,' I said, and told her what he had said. 'So you see, there is a ready-made off-the-hook hater. A man with a motive, and one who, incidentally, messes around with business consultants, and perhaps even, industrial espionage groups.'

'Does K suspect him?'

'K is still in love with his wife, I'd say. That would make him disinclined to spoil her happiness.'

'Is she happy with this duff number?'

'It's surprising how women like duff numbers,' I said, and grinned at her. 'They seem to like the two-faced. A lover to fuss her and son for her to fuss over.'

'Your philosophy is out,' she said. 'I know the type, but it isn't everybody. I prefer a man.'

'I prefer a woman. I went through the other flats. They were all open when I came. I can't think why unless it was the owners ran out in a hurry.'

She had one of my cigarettes.

'Look you've done a lot of this kind of thing, haven't you?'

'I've been pitchforked into some situations. The trouble is, once you start you can't get out of it. There's always somebody who remembers you.'

'Who suggested LOHM to you, anyway?'

'A respectable copper from the Yard said it was good. But to start with it was my old club, now defuncting. The secretary dropped me a line with the bad news and the name of this place. For shooting, that was, not for getting mixed up in things.'

'So that somebody could have known that you would come here sooner or later?'

'What are you guessing, little one? It's new to me.'

'If you were involved with Kilgallen in this — '

'Hang on! I never met Kilgallen till I walked in here.'

'But you both have a lot of money. He says so. He thinks that could be a link. And, you see, you were invited to come here, weren't you? Somebody put you up to it?'

'But a club secretary! I know him well! What the hell could he want to get me into this? How could he know it would happen, anyway?'

'Honest people can be pressurised,' she said quietly. 'And after all, what did the message actually say?'

I told her.

'There are other pistol clubs, you know, specially in London. Why come out to the wilds of Surrey? Why did he recommend us?'

'You're rocking my stability,' I said.

'There's a lot of that going on,' she said, and looked towards the door.

'Don't push me, too,' I said.

'Seeing it's only a couple of hours since I walked in, I've got very fond of you,' she said, cocking her head.

'The very words I've waited for,' I said,

and got hold of her. 'Kiss me Kate.'

I kissed her before she thumped me in the chest and we broke. The brief moment of relief had done me good. I had almost lost the tense depression that had been lurking in my head.

'Tell me the reason for this lovely admission,' I said.

'Surely you can see it?' she said. 'You're not wanted as a witness. You're wanted as a victim. I'm the witness.'

'What — exactly — ?' But I knew before she answered.

'They mean him to kill you as well,' she said. 'The lunatic killer plot. Now do you see?'

It was a cold, prickly moment.

6

We stood looking at each other. The idea of the lunatic killer was chilling, to say very little of it. It was more poignant because I had already suffered a maniac's attack from him, and it wouldn't have taken much more for that to have been a killing.

'You have a dirty mind,' I said.

'It helps one to get the perspective,' she said. 'In this case you need it.'

'He was all right till the phone rang,' I said. 'Then he went off his nut. That could have been his tensions just bursting, like elastic. You can get like that, specially if you worry you *will* get like that.'

'Everything's possible with a fringe nut case,' she said. 'But I'm not convinced.'

'For hours,' I pointed out, 'the poor chap has been aching on the phone starting up again. It could have got like a beetle in his brain. Suddenly it goes.

Eureka! He jumps on it. All will be well, he thinks. Contact with the world at last! The nightmare is over. But no. He gets the call and there isn't one. He stands there and all his hopes and sudden excitements fall about him. He thinks I'm laughing at him. Maybe he thinks everybody's laughing at him, but specially me. Suddenly I represent everybody laughing at him, everybody pointing the finger at him because he's barmy. So — bam! Stop the laughter.'

'You ought to be a psychiatrist,' she said. 'They're often wrong, too.'

'Well, you put it better,' I said. 'Drugs? Where? How?'

'Hypnosis,' she said.

It clicked as if I had thought of it before, but again the objection as to drugs applied to this solution.

'How? By the phone?' I said.

'Well, how else?'

She hoisted herself up and sat on the table, watching me. She was very pretty, very finely coloured, very alive, very desirable, even in that situation. I pushed my mind around to what we were talking about.

'Sound hypnosis,' I said. 'Now you have something. That is the one thing that could be worked in his own car. It could also be worked over the Tannoy here when he got here. It could be worked on a phone. But why doesn't anybody else get the message, too?'

'Kilgallen had treatment. Perhaps hypnosis was part of it. If it was, he was hooked on it anyway. Whoever treated him knew he was a subject and could get him when he wanted.'

'He wouldn't get him in the ordinary way,' I said. 'A man like that would be resistant unless he felt it was for his own good, then he might agree to succumb.'

'And there's a little itchy point,' she said. 'The Tannoy is on in this flat, too. So why the phone?'

'The phone would confine the effects to K., instead of spreading it to me and you.'

'I doubt whether you'd be co-operative, which would give the whole game away, even if it hooked Kilgallen at the same time.'

'You think that fracas was meant to be the lunatic killing?'

'I think they underestimated your will to live,' she said, and laughed briefly.

'It's not nice to think of myself as just an expendable bod.,' I said. 'I had thought of myself in a more impressive role.'

'Who'd get your money if anything happened?' she said.

'What a gay question,' I said. 'I have a few friends around, but no relatives that I know of.'

'No one waiting at the door?' she said.

'You're getting off the beat,' I said. 'This is an industrial set-up designed to ruin Kilgallen and his organisation and incidentally, to wreck yours, too. The reason for wrecking you at the same time as K., seems to be that you — the firm, that is — know a damned sight more about K's troubles than we have thought so far.'

'But this was his first time here. He meant to open the books today.'

'Perhaps your firm wasn't aware how much they did know. They'd know it, but it might not be connected with the K business.'

'Well, we can't be sure of that till we get out of here,' she said.

And then an idea came.

'Have you got any diamonds up here? A ring or something?'

She slid off the table.

'Come and see,' she said.

We sorted out a ring and Kilgallen came and watched while I tried to cut the window. I made a circle all right, I couldn't help that, but this whole set-up had been designed to defeat people who tried to saw circles with diamond cutters. I kept grinding the diamond round and round until the glass started busting up the setting. Then I tried the little hammer.

Kilgallen turned away in disgust even before I chucked in. We went to the trade door which had a fire escape outside, but the glass in the door panel was wire mesh stuff, uncuttable.

Suddenly the phone rang. Sheila and I were alone by the trade door. We looked at each other a minute as if the shock had paralysed us, then we both started off and ran for the nearest phone in the bedroom.

The ringing stopped several seconds before we got there. I snatched up the phone and it was dead as before. I put it down and looked towards the door to the lounge.

'You get back behind me,' I said.

I still had the hammer in my hand and this time I was going to crack his skull with it. To be honest, that first attack had shaken me more than I cared to think. I went cold at the thought of another one. When it came, and we both thought it must come then — my object would have to be to stop it at once.

She went half-behind me, and I reached round and shoved her hard so that she fell back across the bed. I took a few paces towards the door.

We could hear him breathing hard and strangely, as he had done the first time. Then he muttered something and his heavy footsteps thudded on the carpet.

My whole body was tense and I realised the weakness of that and tried to ease myself, and get my balance moving on my toes. It wasn't easy.

She struggled and got up.

We waited there for the coming of the madman. We could still hear his footfalls, but they were not so loud. Then they seemed to stop altogether, but the carpet was thick and he might have decided to creep rather than thump.

Suddenly there was a thump and a click.

'What the hell?' I said. All sound seemed to have stopped.

'The door!' she yelled abruptly. 'It's the door!'

She ran out of the bedroom into the hallway. I followed her. Everything in the hall was as before, with the door shut fast.

Sheila stopped, turned and stared at me.

'For God's sake, look!' she panted.

She pointed. The lounge doorway was empty. The girl's body had gone. I went into the room and looked round. Empty.

She leaned back against the wall and gave a breathless, helpless sort of laugh.

'He's gone!' she gasped. 'Taken the body!'

I ran through the flat to make sure he hadn't gone through the bedroom behind us, carrying her. But we were alone in the place. When I got back she was working the handle of the door as if to try and break it off.

'He must have had a key all the time!' she said.

'No, no, no,' I said, trying to convince myself. 'I feel sure he wasn't kidding us. He isn't the type. If he'd had a key he would have gone long before now.'

'It was the message?'

'It must have been. This time the message was to get the girl and walk out. The door was opened for him. Which spoils the idea of the lunatic killer striking again. Good luck to that one. I can do without it.'

'We look a couple of twits,' she said.

'Fortunately, there's no one to see.'

I sat down on a chest.

'Perhaps the next act,' I said, 'is that somebody comes in and says none of this ever happened at all.'

'Why should they?'

'I was thinking along the hypnosis

suggestion lines. Step by step the build-up to make you disbelieve yourself. That's partly what's been happening to Kilgallen. With him it's worked. Why not give a good thing a second run?'

She went into the lounge.

'The broken chair's here still.'

'I was a damn fool not to have gone for him, instead of waiting for him to come,' I said. 'Cowardice never pays in the long run.'

She came back into the hall.

'It was slick, that act,' she said. 'When we expected him to react as before he goes and does something way out and gets out, which is what we thought was impossible.'

'Does it strike you, darling, that there is a very uncomfortable conclusion to be drawn from the act, as you call it?'

'What?'

'It couldn't have worked if we'd been in the lounge with him,' I said. 'So they must have known he was alone there. Which means that they can see in here.'

She drew a breath, held it and let it go.

'Crummy!' she said. 'I hadn't realised that!'

'Well, where's the hidden eye?' I said. 'Let's look.'

We searched the room completely and there wasn't a knot-hole for a camera anywhere. The room was tight as a drum. We searched the other rooms and the hall and there was no peephole anywhere.

'Then it's just got to be the windows,' I said.

We went to the lounge window and looked out.

'Come to think,' she said, 'Kilgallen was always standing here staring out.'

'Yes, indeed!' I said.

We stared out. The landscape stretched in a wide panorama without a building in sight. There were clumps of elms and beeches and the woods which hid the sight of any man-made eruptions round-about. The road ran to the right with a solitary line of poles for the phone or juice, or both.

'A person couldn't see up from the ground,' she said. 'He'd see only the ceiling — unless Kilgallen signalled.'

'Keep thinking of K as the victim for the time being. We get too many variables if he's going to be an enemy as well. He looks out here. Somewhere the watcher is hiding and holds K's eye, whether he knows it or not. Do you hitch that idea?'

'Could do,' she said. 'You mean someone up in a tree?'

'Someone up a tree with the binocs, watching.'

'So they can see us now.' She turned away and got a cigarette. 'But they're pretty sure we can't see them.'

'They have the advantage of camouflage. I can't see a hair of anybody.'

What we didn't think of was that we were dealing with — or might be — a combination used to industrial espionage. Bugging, they say. That's for listening. But watch cameras are bugs, too. This hit me when we had almost gone cross-eyed looking out of the window into the trees.

'The line down there,' I remember saying. 'The line on the posts. Telephone?'

'Yes. The thick wire underneath is the electric supply. Owing to squeezes of all sorts, we're still locally an under-developed country. It's not a busy road.' She sighed. 'As you can see.'

'If you had a limpet box up near the top of one of those poles,' I said, 'and it had a camera and other electronics within, you could get close circuit television reception, and you could also get jingle mechanism to interrupt the lines to here and ring bells and send signals when you wanted.'

'Well, if they can see us, why not do something to mislead?' she said. 'Put on a performance that would lead them to think we're not so bothered as we bloody well are.'

'I could make love to you,' I said. 'That would put them off the track.'

'Suppose it put me off the track, too?'

'I'd like that.'

'I've always thought the very time to be hugged in a man's arms is when I'm scared to blitherings and he is the strength that will rescue me.'

'This could be now.'

She smiled.

'You're stupid,' she said.

What broke that up was not me giving in, but a sound from out in the hall like somebody using a key in the door. I ran. So did she. I stood one side of the door, she stood the other.

Nothing happened.

After a full minute I tried the handle. The door was still locked. We relaxed, sighing.

'It was something,' I said. 'I'm sure it was a key. There's nothing else here and nobody to make a noise.'

But there came a soft shiffing noise. We spun round to the door again. Nothing seemed to happen, then something white grew under the door. It formed into an envelope, and when it was almost clear of the crack, stopped.

She picked it up. I put my eye to the keyhole, but those good locks don't let much light through. I didn't see anything.

'What is it?' I said.

'It's a letter from Perpignan,' she said, and handed it to me.

'It's *the* letter,' I said. 'The one I saw.

The one you didn't. It's been ripped. Somebody read it.'

I pulled the letter out and unfolded the single sheet.

Headed, 'Boucel et Cie, Perpignan,' it was very brief.

'What's it say?' she said.

'In French,' I said. 'In English it says, 'Police have taken Villa Trieste. House surrounded. No one allowed in. Do not telephone. Write. Boucel. H.''

'Who's it addressed to?' she said.

'John Marsh,' I said. 'I wonder if Villa Trieste is Kilgallen's place?'

'But what has Villa Trieste to do with us?' she said. 'What's the connection? I never head of Boucel et Cie. Let me look.'

She looked.

'It doesn't say dear anybody,' she said.

'But the envelope's addressed to John Marsh, LOHM,' I said.

'But is that the letter that was in it? Can you tell?'

'It fits. I haven't any microscopes to see if the stamp's gone through to the notepaper.'

'Why would the gendarmes grab a

house, surround it, cut it off?'

'Murder. Something like that. I seem to remember a French aircraft man called Marc had Kilgallen's place. This Marc, you said, had been in touch with you. He was coming to see Marsh. It ties up so much I'd bet this villa is Kilgallen's.'

'But it makes it sound as if John has been up to something we know nothing about.'

'Is that against the rules?'

'Yes. If one keeps a thing to himself, then if anything happens nobody else can help. Our system is that business is discussed between the four of us, so that no matter where one may be, he or she is available to deal with some part of the affair. That is the whole basis of John's organisation.'

'But you've said that there are some things you don't know about.'

'I've been away for some hours. What I would normally do is check up on the secret files in the office. I've had no chance.'

'This letter must be meant for Kilgallen, not John Marsh. There could have been two letters, one Marsh's and one Kilgallen's. The notes have been switched in the envelopes, that's all.'

' 'Don't phone,'' she said. 'It sounds as if the addressee is involved in whatever the police are on to.'

'But is it possible for a man like Kilgallen to be mixed up in something the police would be after? His position isn't a fake. His organisation is too well known to be any of a phoney. How can a man like that be involved in some shady business that suddenly gets snatched by the police?'

'There is a way,' she said.

'Give it.'

'This man *is* Kilgallen, is he? Have you ever met K?'

'No. I recognised him from photographs.'

'Not enough evidence, is it? Suppose this fellow is some double, just a likeness. Suppose he isn't the big businessman but a junky who's been coached in the part?'

'A very interesting thought,' I said. 'But what in hell would these operators want to lock up their own catspaw for?'

'They let him out,' she said. 'Remember?'

'Coached in the part,' I said, trying to remember. 'But he gave a hell of a lot of details. They all came out at the right times. And there was a real feeling when he talked about his wife.'

'That makes a stumbler, but I still wouldn't ditch the idea.'

We went back into the lounge and looked out of the window.

'I'm frayed out with this,' I said. 'Exhausted. If there's one thing I cannot stand it's doing nothing. It ties me up like a rope. I'm only any good when there's some action. In action, things look after themselves. Cooped up here like a couple of nitwits is just the wrong treatment for my temperament.'

'Perhaps they know that,' she said. 'Perhaps they know you very well. Is that possible?'

'How the hell do I know, as I don't know who they are?'

'Don't get so ragged.'

'Can I help it? I'm out of smoke.'

'I'll get some,' she said.

She walked out of the doorway into the hall. I heard her stop dead and turned round. She was looking towards the flat entrance. Then she looked towards me.

'Observe the bloody miracle,' she said.

I went into the hall and looked at the flat door. It was wide open. The vestibule landing beyond was empty. Everything was as quiet as a tomb.

'Don't trust it,' I said. 'Just get the cigarettes.'

She went away and came back with a new packet. I went to the doorway and looked out, along the walls either side. Then I went out and looked behind the big sofas. Then I went to the landing rail and looked down the wide, green carpeted stairs. Nobody. Not a sound.

Back in the hallway we lit cigarettes.

'This is a madhouse,' I said. 'Let's go down, but watch it, every step.'

We went down, keeping quiet and watching so that nobody could step out behind us, or at the sides, or ahead. We were in no hurry.

Especially were we in no hurry to die.

She led the way into Marsh's office. It

was all tidy and bare, as she had said. The diary had gone.

'Let's try the outside doors,' I said. 'We want to get out first. Solving anything can come later.'

We went to the garden door by the gymnasium. Locked as firmly as the flat door had been. We tried the exits from the gym itself. Locked.

'Where do we keep the keys?' I said.

We went back into Marsh's office and she did a fancy twist trick with one of the drawer handles. The drawer came out but kept on coming out till the first drawer part was fully out and a second compartment was disclosed.

It was an empty secret compartment.

'Gone,' she said.

'I'm surprised,' I said. 'Let's try the main door.'

We went without hope and were duly rewarded with nothing.

'I'm sick of these burglar-proof outfits,' I said.

'I never thought it was that efficient,' she said.

'Listen, there must be some tools

around somewhere down here.' I brightened up at the idea.

'Yes! Down in the cleaners' cupboards. Of course! Boiler wrenches and things. You know.'

We ran down to the cupboards which were to one side of the gym entrance. There were three.

They were all locked.

'Great stink!' she said furiously. 'It's been done deliberately! I shall scream! I shall scream the bloody place flat!'

I got hold of her and held her still, though she struggled as if she wanted to tear her hair. I kissed her and then for a minute or two the whole thing was lifted out of the prison.

Then she broke away.

'You do choose the occasion, don't you?' she said.

'So do you,' I said. 'What else is there to do?'

She went off into the offices, one after the other and tried the phones. They were all dead.

'Why don't they show up?' she cried. 'What are they afraid of?'

'They don't want to spoil the tension. At present they've organised a fine build-up. We're slowly going off our nuts. Let's try the flats.'

We tried Marsh's: locked. The ones upstairs were open as they had been when I first arrived. We went through them one after the other.

'Mary left in a rush,' Sheila said as we went through the untidy flat. 'Looks as if something happened to make her go like that.'

In Jane's flat everything was tidy. But Sheila stopped in the bedroom and picked a fine leather satchel bag off the dressing table.

'Jane, too. It must have been a sudden rush.'

'Does she always carry this bag?' I said.

'We all do. They contain valuable equipment.'

She opened it. There were ordinary things in it, but the centre purse pushed them all aside and showed up a false bottom. Inside there was a two-way radio.

'I see,' I said. 'So that normally, even with an urgent call, she would naturally grab up this bag and then run?'

'That's the order of the thing,' Sheila said.

'This only adds to the coffee and cigarette in Marsh's study,' I said. 'But what the hell was it that called them out so that they forgot their habits?'

And then memory came back clear above the emotion which was getting a kind of worm's hold on me.

'That damn bag wasn't here when I first came,' I said. 'I remember, the room was clear. There were just the brushes and things on the dressing table. No bag.'

'You heard somebody in one of the flats, running water,' she said. 'This is the last flat to go in and there weren't any signs of water run in the others.'

She went across to the bathroom door and turned the handle. She pushed. It was locked on the inside.

She knocked and called out, 'Jane! Jane!' As if there was a desperate hope the missing girl might be in there.

Nobody answered.

'It's no good,' she said, and started to go out.

'Before you go,' I said.

She stopped and looked back at me. I pointed to the handbag.

'Try the radio,' I said.

She hissed as if cursing herself for being so worked up as not to have thought of that one. She tried it and repeated a call sign three times, then flipped over to receive.

A voice came out of the little speaker in the bag. We almost stuck our heads inside.

'Now then,' the voice said, 'keep those stomachs well in. Hold it! Now push the head back, keeping the shoulders level, chin in to the chest. That's it — '

'What in hell's that?' I said.

'It's John. Taking a fitness class.' She sighed.

'Keep those stomachs in, gentlemen. That's it now — ' There was a scrunch and then the same voice said, 'Yes, I understand the difficulty, Monsieur. Yes, indeed. But the villa, I understand, is the property of Lord Kilgallen, which will complicate the operation considerably ... I do not see how you can make a killing so far away as that, and there is always the danger of a tip-off. However, I will do the best I can for you . . . Yes. On Saturday.'

The transmission ended.

'It's a tape,' she said, incredulously. 'A tape.'

'A tape of your partner hatching some nefarious plot with the Frenchman who had the villa. And now the villa has been taken by the police!'

'It's impossible!' she said. 'We should have known.'

'You should have known.' I underlined the should. 'But it looks as if your partner has been operating on his own.'

'You keep going back to that suggestion!' she flared up.

'Why not? I don't imagine anyone outside could have known the secret back of the drawer in his desk, to name just one thing.'

7

'Anyway,' I said, 'the chat mentions Saturday and it links the villa with Kilgallen and I should say, Marc. Kilgallen and Marc were expected here today.'

'So there's nothing very extraordinary,' she said, defensively.

'Except that the letter was posted yesterday about noon at the latest,' I said. 'That would be most rapid, also. It was probably sent earlier. But Kilgallen didn't ring to make an appointment until 5 p.m. A call which didn't get here, we have betted.'

'So you reckon K isn't involved?'

'Except as a victim.'

'You keep thinking of him as the victim,' she said, sharply. 'Suppose he isn't? Suppose he was in dead trouble before he decided to come here. Have you thought of that?'

'But his position — '

'You know how many men in apparently topdog positions suddenly crash. There's nothing strange about that these days. The ten million pound firm can dissolve overnight and the police rounding up the chairman next morning.'

'I am aware of present frailties. But such weaknesses rarely apply to manufacturing concerns. Theirs is a solid business. If they fail, others help, or move in and take over. There's always something there, something left to sell.'

'Suppose it's all in hock?'

'There are consultants who can arrange something. The amount of hock is always known because it concerns actual property. There's the check on hire purchase, bank loans, operating debts. It isn't money juggling. It's making something.'

It was then that we heard someone talking.

We were in the main corridor, and the voice came as a shock after the long quiet. It seemed to be carrying on a conversation but we couldn't catch the words. It ended with a laugh, but no other voice replied.

'It's in the bar,' Sheila said, and moved quickly towards its open doors.

I followed her. At the doorway we both stopped and stared in.

Kilgallen was at a table, bending over it, pouring champagne into two glasses. Across the table from him sat the dead nude, like a ghastly wax model propped in position.

'My God!' Sheila whispered.

'He's gone,' I said. 'It's snapped this time.'

I felt very bad, apart from sick at the awful sight. I felt bad for him. My feelings had gone beyond the depths of pity almost to a personal grief. I can't explain the depth of feeling Kilgallen created in me. It was akin to watching an animal suffering without understanding, but suffering in quiet patience.

Sheila stayed at the door, and I saw her turn away. I went in. Kilgallen looked up and waved the bottle.

'Join us,' he said. 'Get a glass.'

There was a queer look in his eye, and kind of glint which I had seen before. When he had tried to kill me.

Till then I had thought of trying to soothe him, lead him away from his macabre party, make him see he was making things far worse for himself in every way.

But I saw that his was not the mood to receive such advice. That look came close to saying out loud, 'Go on, say I'm mad, just say it and I'll show you.'

I got a glass and came back to the table. For a moment I thought he would get me with the bottle clubwise, but he laughed as if pleased with me and poured some wine.

'Bring the lady,' he said. 'This is a celebration. She is not dead after all, as you see. She is drinking with us.'

Some kind of a shudder hit me and I nearly let the glass go. In reverse I nearly crushed it in my hand.

There is one thing about madness which is near you and controlled only by a very fine thread; it is very bad for your nerves.

I turned and looked at Sheila and nodded. She made a slight grimace, but she came in. I got another glass. He filled it for her. We remained standing. Thus far was as much as we could go. We couldn't sit down with that corpse.

'You were lucky to be let out,' I said. 'It helped to clear things up.'

He responded to the jockeying.

'Yes. He came just in time. 'Come down, bring the girl', he said.' Kilgallen stopped and frowned.

'Who?' I asked.

'Henri.' He looked surprised I didn't know.

'Marc?'

'Of course.'

'I thought he was in Perpignan.'

'He had to leave.'

'I'd forgotten,' I said, playing cool. 'The police took over the villa.'

'Yes,' Kilgallen said. 'It comes at a very bad time. Poor Henri. But he was taking too many risks. It's all very well, this tightrope walking, but if the wire slacks one has to jump.'

He was walking about, gesturing with the glass. He assumed that we knew all about Henri and the affair at Perpignan.

'It was lucky he got here in time to let

you out,' Sheila said.

She seemed easy, but I could see the tenseness in her attitude, and she kept her very blue eyes on Kilgallen and well above the dead girl.

'I knew he would come,' Kilgallen said.

'Where is he now?' Sheila said, looking round. 'He ought to be celebrating with us.'

Kilgallen stood still, and his eyes got far away and began to darken with puzzlement. He touched his forehead.

'Where did he go?' he said, talking to himself. 'Where the devil did he go?'

Suddenly he marched past us to the open doorway and stopped there looking up and down the corridor.

'Henri. Henri!' He shouted in a voice like a bull's. 'Where are you? Henri!'

His powerful voice echoed, and that was all the answer he got.

'He couldn't have got out,' I said. 'The whole place is locked up.'

'Henri has the keys,' Kilgallen said, without realising what he was giving away. 'Where did he go?'

'Of course he has the keys,' said Sheila.

'He let you out of the flat. Did you unlock the door for us, or was it Henri?'

Kilgallen didn't answer but walked out. He yelled his way through the building calling for Henri.

'He's gone,' she said. 'It's awful.'

'Or is it still hypnosis?' I said. 'He thinks he saw Henri. Did he? Do you think he did?'

'I just couldn't think straight, with her sitting there,' she said, and choked a little. 'Surely he must have seen Henri to go off shouting for him like that?'

'He might have been told to see Henri,' I said. 'In his present state of mind the hypnotic influence must be getting easier and easier to throw at him.'

'He says Henri had to run from France because of the police being there. Did they throw him that idea, too? Or did he see that letter?'

'The letter doesn't mention anyone. It could concern a servant.'

'But both he and John Marsh knew something was fishy about the villa.'

We heard his occasional bellow in the distance.

'Marc is an industrialist who uses equipment provided by Kilgallen's plants,' I said. 'It isn't that he is being framed as well, is it? K won't say what was worrying him about his works. Somebody is spying on something there. Suppose it is to do with aircraft navigation or some such. Marc could be concerned with the espionage as well as K.'

'What happened to his damn brief-case?' she said.

'It got took,' I said. 'That was an essential part of this particular plot. It was took because it had a direct clue as to who the spy was.'

'You don't think Kilgallen knew who it was?'

'I think he was 'didn't-know-at-all'. Otherwise why should he come to you? But I think there was something in his papers that could have meant an early disclosure.'

'Which ties it to what we thought, that it must be someone in his offices. No one outside could get a look at his papers.'

'It might also mean it was someone

who didn't want to lose a valuable position,' I said. 'Anyone outside wouldn't care. He would be paid by someone further outside still.'

'What a pity we're locked in,' she said. 'It's trying to solve something by remote control.'

'A *Marie Roget*.'

'Starting with a *Marie Celeste*,' she said. 'Both French. Or is that too remote for our control?'

We heard Kilgallen coming back, walking fast, angrily. He came in the door.

'He must have gone,' he said.

'That's funny,' I said. 'When you had arranged to talk business with him?'

He let that sly one hit his wicket.

'Yes,' he said. 'Obviously he must mean to come back.'

'Do you speak French?' Sheila said.

'No. Can't get my tongue round it.'

'But you must have someone in your offices who does?' she said. 'You do business with foreign firms.'

'That's one thing I let out — to Blackhurst,' he said. 'He speaks four

European languages. His mother was Hungarian.'

'Who's Blackhurst?' I said.

'My wife's husband,' he said, bitterly.

We didn't push that. The link was now solid enough not to need more hammering.

He seemed to be coming out of his daze for he suddenly looked past us and saw the girl in the velvet seat.

'My God!' he said, and turned his back. 'Did I do that?'

He walked out. Some way down the corridor he just stopped and stood there, looking at the floor.

'Surely he can see it must be Blackhurst, his spy?' she whispered.

'It seems too obvious,' I said. 'Besides, if K's description of him as a feckless rogue is not just jealousy, then he's the sort that would sell anybody anything any time. Hardly the secret sort.'

'I bet he's to do with this, anyway. He'd be in a good position, knowing K wouldn't give him away for fear of hurting his ex.'

'Yes. But I'm getting more and more

hooked on this hypnosis jazz of yours,' I said. 'In which case, it links back to the breakdown and the nursing home he went to.'

'Which argues that this plot started a long time back,' she said. 'The sort of thing that gradually builds up till everything's ready, and then it's almost sure of success.'

'If you were meant to be implicated a long time back,' I said, 'then it's more than likely the implicator came here and registered as a fitness class man.'

'Could be,' she said, frowning. 'But I know them all.'

'He told me his breakdown was two years back,' I said. 'That's a long time to incubate a plot. It's also a long time to keep on doing a fitness course.'

'We do have them stay on,' she said. 'Our type of customer is away a good deal, and he attends when he's back at the office.'

'So it wouldn't be unusual to have one two years old?'

'I wouldn't know,' she said. 'Two years back I was modelling. I became a partner here fourteen months back.'

She shivered. 'I can't stand here any more,' she said, and walked into the corridor.

I followed her. On our left the big glass double doors looked up the long drive between the lawns.

A man was walking along that drive towards the doors. He reached the steps and came up them. I ran to the doors, but I knew it wouldn't be any good shouting for the double glass would kill the sound.

He stared through the glass at me, then up to the top of the doors, then down, then to either side. I waved and beckoned to him.

He took no notice whatever. He seemed to be looking for the bell. He found it. I saw him press it. No sound came in the building.

He stared through the glass at me. I waved frantically and shouted. He looked aside and pressed the bell again.

I looked behind me. Kilgallen had gone. I saw Sheila, running like mad, disappearing round the corner of the stairs.

Bewildered by her flight, I turned back to the man. He stared through at me. I waved and gestured and shouted. Then he shrugged, turned and went down the steps and away down the drive.

★ ★ ★

It had been just another silent act from a nightmare. I remember standing there, stunned, incredulous. Then I turned round and ran back to the stairs.

She was at the top, breathless, her golden hair hanging over one eye as she stared down.

'They've locked all the bloody doors again!' she called down. 'He'll get away!'

I began to get the drift and looked back to the glass doors. The man had stopped in doubt to look back at the building. Then once more he shrugged and went on to the gateway.

'Those downstairs doors and windows are one-way glass,' she panted, coming down the stairs. 'You can see out. Nobody can see in. But upstairs — oh hell! I could have signalled from a window there!'

The nightmare was explained, by this one more supercaution in the architecture. It still left a weird impression of having been looked right through, as if I'd been a ghost.

'What happened to K?' I said.

'He went into the gym.'

So we went to the gym also. He was leaning against a vaulting horse, head on his arms, like a man dozing on a rope in a flophouse.

As I saw him it gave me a shock, and I got a depression cloud in me that made me think he was dead. When he moved I felt a sweep of relief.

These feeling were a sure sign this day was getting the better of my nerves. The long hours of queer suspense and almost lunatic irrelevance, the tension of feeling something big should happen but didn't, all massed up together, and pulled my nerves apart.

Kilgallen looked round, still leaning on the horse.

'Has he gone?' he croaked.

'Who? The man at the door?' I said.

'Yes.'

'You hid from him?' Sheila said, staring. 'What for? Who is he?'

'Blackhurst,' Kilgallen said.

After all K had said about the deadbeat, to find he was frightened of him was an unexpected twist. Like the rest of it, it made no sense.

'Did he know you came here?' I asked.

'He must have found out,' Kilgallen said.

'He looked pretty blank,' I said. 'An innocent waiting for someone to come to the door. And the way he walked off didn't look as if his call was important. Have you ever mentioned LOHM to him?'

'I didn't know about LOHM till a couple of days ago.'

'Who mentioned it then?'

'My secretary, Mrs. Jave. She knew that I'd been worried and I got her to look up some — consultants in this line.'

'Who told her what we are?' Sheila said.

'Mrs. Jave is a very intelligent secretary. She has been with me for ten years. You need waste no time suspecting her.'

'Does she get on with Blackhurst?' I said.

'All women do,' he said.

'Was he married before he met your wife?'

'No.'

A possible line went up the spout in an ex-wife, needing money, in the background. But it still left the possibility of girl-friends round about.

'Have you ever had him watched?' Sheila said.

It was a shrewd one, that, and one that jolted him a little more than somewhat. He hesitated over answering it.

'Yes,' he said at last.

'What was the result?' she said.

'Nothing that I didn't know.'

'But what was it you did know?'

'What does one expect to know about ladies' men?' He turned on her. It was nasty.

She came back quicker than he spat.

'Where's your wife now?'

That caught him when he had his guard up on another angle, because he just stood there. He didn't know what to say. It was painfully obvious.

'I don't know,' he said at last. 'I'm not married to her any more.'

'You must have an idea,' the persistent female said. 'She still asks you for money, doesn't she?'

'I give her money!' he shouted. 'I make an allowance.'

'That's not enough. Her husband needs more than she gets.'

She was lashing him.

'Easy, easy!' I said.

'I want to know!' She never looked at me at all, but kept her eyes on him, dead on.

'I don't know where she is,' he repeated.

'Is she alive?' Sheila said.

There was a dead silence, from me as well. He looked back at her. It looked as if the stuffing had been knocked out of him. He sagged. He became almost deflated.

'I hope so,' he said.

It was dramatic. To me it proved the man's innocence. I didn't want to know any more. Kilgallen was a beaten man; had been beaten by his wife. He had wanted her all along, but she had beaten him off. She had got her own back for his putting his life's work first, and in doing it, she had broken him up.

I thought I could see it all. The breakdown had not been overwork, but her.

One of my troubles is sentiment.

I didn't want to look at it any more. If we hadn't been locked in this place we shouldn't have had to look on at this harrowing sight.

The light was coming in from roof lights. I looked up, and then I remembered.

Once I'd broken into a drill hall by way of the skylights and the gym apparatus which had reached almost up to them.

My eye caught the wall ladders going up to the ceiling but not outwards to the lights. But there was a climbing rope hanging from a steel joist about four feet short of the middle light.

Although the building was very modern in many directions, it seemed there was no special new way of opening lights from below. These had the old worms and steel quadrants for raising and lowering the lights. The only new thing was that, instead of cords operating the worms, there were small electric motors.

'Open the lights, Sheila,' I said, pointing up. 'Where's the button?'

'On the wall.'

She went to the switch panel and pressed a couple of buttons. Nothing happened.

'Try the lights,' I said.

She did. Again nothing happened.

'The juice is off,' I said. 'That's why the bells didn't ring when Blackhurst pressed ... Look, I'm going up there and try to work the worms by hand. It might be a way out. If you can climb a rope.'

'I can,' she said.

'I wait till I walk out,' Kilgallen said, then added, 'or get carried.'

'Cheer up,' I said, and unloosed the rope from the wall hook.

I didn't hope for too much from this expedition. The operators had thought of everything so thoroughly, it didn't seem likely they had forgotten a way out. But it was something to do. Anything was better than this aimless wait till nobody knew when.

My rope climbing was rusty and with a bad shoulder, putrid. Half-way up I nearly gave in and slid back down again. I rested a while, and Sheila kept calling out was I all right. I kept my breath and went on up.

At the beam I hoicked myself over and sat there looking at the light gears above me. It looked as if the quadrants could be lifted off the worms and pushed up free.

Standing up would be tricky on a three-inch joist and nothing to get hold of to steady on. I thought of Kilgallen's tightrope similes. If I overbalanced on this stand-up job I would hit the floor forty feet below with my head. It was a lovely floor. But I had a lovely head.

I sat some time working out how I was going to raise myself without overbalancing. I tried all fours, but it was too narrow a beam. I thought of standing up suddenly and grabbing the gears, but I couldn't get my feet on to the beam together without putting myself broadside and toppling over.

168

Sometimes ideas come when it seems too late. One came then.

Reaching under me I got the rope a foot below the hook and began pulling it up. The first part was awkward, for I almost overbalanced with it, but the more I got across my lap the easier it got.

I pulled the lot up, then looped the end over and tried to sling it over the nearest quadrant. I missed five times. The sixth time it hooked on.

It wasn't to hang on to with any weight, but it made a balance guide. Very gingerly I began to raise myself on my feet, guiding my hand along the rope as a steady.

The gears came within reach and I got a good hard grip. At the same time I let my breath go in a whistle.

After a moment's rest I shoved the light upwards. It gave. I jammed the end of the quadrant into the worm gear guard so that the light stayed open a foot. Then I hauled myself up through the slot and on to the roof.

For a half-minute I just lay on the asphalt feeling the great wind of freedom aerating my nerves.

'Are you all right?' Sheila's voice called up from below.

'Okay,' I bawled back, and then looked around.

There was no escape handrail to be seen anywhere. Three sides of the roof dropped sheer to the ground. The fourth butted up against the wall of the flat and office block. That wall reared up twenty feet with no holds on it.

A tour of the parapet showed nowhere I could tie a rope on. That was a pity, for I had a rope handy, a thing one doesn't often have.

Pacing the distance to the nearest bit of the parapet made seven feet. Guessing the length of the rope at thirty-five, and adding the four feet down to the beam to seven I got twenty-four feet.

Which would leave a drop of about sixteen, which would be manageable if the landing wasn't hard.

Looking down I was relieved to find the grass came up to the wall, except for a small gulley about six inches wide.

Back at the light I unfastened the rope

end from the gearing and told the two below what I was going to do.

Of course, anyone else nearby could have heard it, too, but I didn't think there was anyone nearby.

The rope kept getting caught in the quadrant arm when I pulled it and wasted more time. Ropes you climb are not very thin and pliable, in fact this one was tough and almost untractable.

I got it all out and slung the end over the parapet. It snaked away from me then as if keen to be over the side. It went on snaking away, and then I saw the cut end go snaking away after the rest. In a second the whole rope had gone.

Some things take a moment or two to soak in. I think I just stood there like a fool, watching where the rope had gone over.

Then I understood part of it, anyway, and dived at the light to look down. The cut bit of rope was still swinging on its hook below the beam. I could see the frayed strands quite clearly where a blade had gone right through.

But no one was on the beam.

No one was in the gym below, either. 'Sheila! Sheila!'

I shouted in good spirit because first, I couldn't make out where she and Kilgallen had gone, and more important, why. At a crucial moment like that, when they should have been waiting to see if I could get away with it — and save them after hours of tension — at that moment they'd run away.

Mystery one. Mystery two was who and how had cut the rope.

The only distinctly clear point about the whole situation was that I was now stuck on the roof without a way down to the ground either inside or outside.

I went to the parapet and looked down at the rope coiled up on the grass. Then I went back to the skylight and looked down through at the empty gym.

And while I was kneeling there, I heard a shot.

8

The shot didn't hit anything and I didn't hear it travelling, so it could have been any old shot. It was just a solitary crack, which echoed in the woods.

Cautious to the end, I crouched by the parapet and peered around. It could have been somebody having a pot shot in the woods, but the whole day of uneasiness did not let me believe that.

If they could watch from up in the trees they could also fire from there.

The quiet of the late afternoon remained undisturbed for a while. Keeping doubled up, I made back for the skylight where it opened up, angling into the air.

Thus the slope of steel and glass was between me and the trees where I guessed the watch had been kept from. My other guess was that, as the rest of the glass in the place was bullet-and-diamond-stopping, I guessed this would be too.

A bullet pinged on a steel corner of the light and screamed away in agony. A bit second later the sound of the shot came.

Almost with it a large hole suddenly cracked through one of the panes near my head and powdered glass sprayed out almost at leisure after the initial shock.

I didn't wait for the sound of that shot, but heaved myself over the edge of the light and down on to the beam inside.

The empty gym seemed a hundred feet down from that narrow beam. The cut rope end swung uneasily on its ring under the joist.

The beam ran to the wall either end and reached down to within about ten feet of a set of polished wall bars which ran down to the floor.

If I could get along the beam to that end, there was a chance of making a jump for the bars. It wouldn't be pleasant, and it was likely to fail altogether, but someone had cut the rope.

That meant someone who didn't like me was also within the building. I could be shot at from inside as well as outside.

I was going to let my hold on the light

edge go when I saw a machete sticking into the plaster board of the ceiling just on the edge of the light.

That had been the instrument which had cut the rope. Slung from somewhere down below, and judging from the angle it stuck into the boards, from the double doors leading into the main corridor.

I got hold of it, and after some twisting and wrenching, got it free. Then I stuck it into the waistband of my slacks and prepared for my journey to the wall.

I couldn't walk it. The way was too narrow. I got down on all fours monkey fashion on a branch, then let my feet and body down until I was hanging by the hands. Then I started to hand walk.

Normally it would have been fairly easy but my shoulder had gone solid with pain and made the whole side of my body feel stiff and got in the way of the swinging rhythm.

The silence stayed below. I kept an eye on the doorway down there as best I could, though lord knows what I could have done if anyone had turned up there.

At the wall I just hung and tried to

175

judge the drop to the bars. Being close up against the wall they offered nothing to land on. To get hold of them meant dropping against the bars and trying to scrabble a hold on them somehow, so long as it stopped my long downward curve.

Hanging by the hands is no position to judge an accurate landing anywhere. I swung until I reckoned I would drop against the bars if I let go, and then I dropped.

I hit the bars all right, smack flat except for the feet. The thump partly winded me and I missed the grip with my hands as I fell outwards and backwards.

The only saving thing was that my feet were between the bars, just. Remembering what I had been told by a gentleman who earns his living slinging himself around on trapezes, I managed to kick upwards.

That hooked my toes under the bar above the one I'd got my feet on. I went down with a crash all right, full fourteen stone swinging on a loose hinge and with a six-foot moment arm I got it smack in the back.

I had to hang there a few seconds shaking the stars out of my vision. The machete came out of my belt, almost sliced my nose off and dug into the floor at the bottom.

Hanging there till my head felt it would burst with the blood I got a proper hold with my hands, let my feet go and swung out and down letting go about five feet up, which was an easy land.

The same silence was all around when as I got my balance, bent and got the broad knife from the floor then looked around me.

It had occurred to me that if the skylight glass was bulletable, then the precautions against burglars getting into the gym might be weaker than the rest of the building.

The double doors to the main corridor were heavy oak, and the foot square glass panels in each were filled with the cast wire stuff, which seemed to bear out my guess.

But there was only one exit from the place and no windows.

That exit was a sort of fire door which we had tried before. It was shut.

I went out into the corridor. Silence everywhere.

I couldn't think what had happened to Sheila and Kilgallen. Either they had run before the knife had been thrown, or they had been forced to go by the knife-thrower.

Except that I had been out there on the roof and the two would most likely have been staring up at the skylight from inside the gym.

The knife, therefore, could have been slung up over their heads and the thrower gone again before they realised what had happened.

Through the day of strange happenings, one thing which had cropped up before in our guesses about what was really going on was the fact that we didn't see anyone.

The doors were locked, unlocked, things taken and put back and no one was seen doing anything.

Kilgallen had suggested an invisible person. I didn't go for that. The trapeze man had let me into a lot of the tricks of his and allied trades. I remembered him talking about illusionist tricks which he also did on the side.

'You watch. You see that nothing happens. An instant later you see it has happened. But yet you saw that it didn't. That's the surprise. What is the secret, then? Something up the sleeve? Hardly ever. Quite unnecessary. Speed is the answer. Just speed. If you can be fast, no one will see you move.'

I think he is a Swede. He clips every sentence with scissors.

Walking along that corridor again, I tried to apply his theory to what had happened. The thing here was that speed could get the man away so far. But he had to have a duck-in place at the end of the fast move.

There must be somewhere we hadn't looked. Somewhere we took for granted.

Then I remembered the soft whine of machinery up in the tankhouse. The lift. Someone had used the lift.

For active people like Sheila and myself, even Kilgallen, the business of getting into a lift, closing the door, pressing the button and getting out later, was somewhat slower than just running up the thirty wide, shallow stairs.

Why a lift with only one floor above?

Either it was mainly intended to get heavy goods upstairs, or there was a floor below as well.

Sheila hadn't mentioned one, but then she was used to the whole place. She knew of it, no doubt, but she would also know that there was no way out of it, which is why it hadn't cropped up.

There was no juice on anywhere else in the building, and the lift indicator wasn't alight. I pressed the button. Nothing seemed to happen. But as I was going to walk away the doors slid open silently.

A light shone inside the grey metal box. I hadn't heard a thing of its coming. It was magnificently soundproofed. That clinched it.

If the X-man was using this lift to be where we didn't think he would be, we shouldn't have heard him moving from floor to floor.

I left it, doors open so nobody could

work it except from where I was, and went through the ground floor looking for the missing pair.

Nothing turned up. I got in the lift and went up. Up there I left the doors open again.

And the doors of all the flats were wide open, too. I was sick of this open-and-shut business. If I caught any joker fooling about with a door I felt like slicing him up with the machete.

Calling out Sheila brought no answer. I got in the lift and poked the Basement button. We slid down. It was very quiet and stopped almost before I realised we'd started. The doors slid open.

Outside them there wasn't a solitary gleam of light anywhere. The lift light was soft and didn't reach out more than a few feet across the floor, like a little apron laid on black.

On my key wallet I always carry a very small light, intended for finding keyholes. Out in that gloom it was like an illuminated pea. I did find a plaster wall and a flush panelled door in it. With that kind of finish I guessed these were extra offices and perhaps file rooms.

As I found the door the light in the lift went out. I turned round very quickly, because I couldn't be sure if the light had failed or the doors, closing, had cut it off. I hadn't heard them, but then, the whole of the machinery was excellent in its silence.

Then somebody spoke. It got me right in the middle of the spine with an ice poker.

'Mr. Blake, I want to talk to you,' it said.

For a moment I hesitated about whether to answer and popped my little light out, as it made me a fair target. I stepped well aside and got my back to the smooth door so nobody could creep up behind.

'You are doing so,' I said.

'You should give up this idiotic search to get out of here.'

'I am the best judge of the idiotic.'

'The doors will be opened at nine. Surely you can wait that long?'

I didn't answer.

'You hear me?'

'I'm just wondering where I've heard your voice before,' I said. 'It's reminiscent.'

'I assure you, we have never met.'

'I didn't say we had. I said I knew your voice. Not exactly as it is, but more as it was. There are a number of people I know well over a telephone but wouldn't know them from Adam if I saw them. I'm sure we've done business.'

That fired it. In my real business as a surveyor I deal largely with architects. I also have long conversations over details with architects and their senior assistants.

The one thing about this building had been a kind of oddness in the design. For all the care taken in the details against intruders it could well have been a bank.

Forgiving the fact that some papers LOHM dealt with would need as careful keeping as a bank's affairs, it still seemed convenient that the precautions could be switched from keeping them out to keeping them in.

The architecture of the building had been used intimately by the secret operators.

Who would know a building as intimately as the architect responsible for it?

I let the idea sink in and drove away from it.

'You just want me to lie still until nine?'

'That is roughly the idea.'

Like mad I wanted to know where Sheila was, but decided not to show an Achilles spot.

'Where's Kilgallen?'

'Out. Surely you didn't think he could keep on taking that strain?'

'I have feared for him all day. Not that he might break up, but that he might cease to believe he could keep on.'

I was just talking to cover up trying to think out a chain of jobs I had done in the last two years. What made it difficult was that I freelance and often take in jobs from larger firms of surveyors. This confuses the line.

But Johnson, Carr and Nephew tend to get a lot of hospital jobs. I have helped them on some, and whittling it down in my head I shaped out two nursing home jobs.

One was near Aberdeen, which I thought would be too far out, and the other, Liston Grange, was in Buckingham.

There it had been an extensive alteration job on an old country house. I had done the variations after the place had been opened for patients. Variations are the differences between what is finally built and what was originally intended to be built. You go and measure up what has been built, then go home and deduct all the original specification which affects that alteration. The balance between these items being what the building owner finally pays.

The links were becoming much clearer. 'What's the idea behind all this pantomime?' I said.

While the voice went on telling me not to bother and just be quiet till nine, I was trying to remember doing that job in Buckingham.

As I recalled incidents of that time I began to see links forging themselves that practically chained me round Kilgallen's neck — if Liston Grange had been the place he went to with his disorder.

Kilgallen and I had both thought our only common element was money. If it was Liston Grange then the whole picture changed drastically. Even shockingly.

It meant I would never get out of this dump, either at nine or any other time.

* * *

'You say he's passed out,' I said. 'What are you going to do about that? Send him back to Liston?'

'Who can tell? It's more likely to be a criminal lunatic asylum. He killed a girl, you remember.'

'I don't remember. I have definite proof that he didn't kill her.'

That stopped the hubbub. There was a long pause before the Tannoy went on speaking.

'What evidence?'

'You're thinking hard, trying to remember what you overlooked, aren't you? Go on thinking. I don't know whether you'll be able to see into my pocket in this light.'

'We are used to bluff, Mr. Blake.'

'I doubt it. When we measure that pause you made on my pocket tape it'll show five inches of nervous shock.'

'You have no tape!'

'You must be a fool to think that. My guess is that Kilgallen was hypnotised over the Tannoy and my tape will show whether he was or not.'

The loudspeaker hissed sharply. I felt good that I was getting this nemo better than he was getting me.

Except that he stood a better chance of getting me in the physical end of the encounter.

'So if you want to be safe at nine,' I said, 'you'd better come and get this tape. There's no other way out for you now.'

'You're a bloody liar!'

'You're a bloody amateur,' I said. 'Stick to making boxes and pricking square holes in them. You're a dead loss as a villain.'

Something happened. It was as if somebody shoved him from the microphone, for there was a soft, confused noise and then nothing but the soft background hiss of the instrument.

Then it started. The funny thing was that there was almost nothing to hear. It was a soft undulation of near-sound, if that can describe this almost completely background hushing. It seemed to have tone, but the harder I listened the more Nothing it became.

But the rhythm of it was there, steadily beating like waves on a constant speed river, or the undulating of a snake's backbone over regular corrugations.

They were the kind of looney comparisons I made when I was trying to work out what it was.

And while I was working it out, I failed to realise it was getting into me. Suddenly I found my head was swaying to the beat of the undulations.

The answer came in then.

It was the old hypnotist's trick of swinging the watch in front of the patient, sending him to sleep, or near it. Only this was doing it by sound.

The lift light came on again. It was a shock in the darkness and momentarily broke the spell of the whispering poison.

I stared at it blankly, glowing in many colours from the shock on my retina, and as the only light in the great darkness I couldn't look anywhere else.

The whispering rhythm was uninterrupted. I began to notice it again and when I did I saw the lift box swinging slowly from side to side, like the watch on the hypnotist's chain.

My common sense told me it wasn't moving, but all my sensory perceptions told me it was. A feeling of a dream state of peace was getting hold of me. Everything began to look easy. All the tensions began to slacken.

It suddenly seemed a splendid thing to let go and rest after the strain of the day. To go into the lift and rise up to the bright air of the afternoon and not to worry any more about Kilgallen and his troubles.

Or about my own. They seemed to be all over. I couldn't work out why they were, or how they had been solved, but I felt as if they had all sunk away down a drain.

I don't remember actually walking

189

towards the lift. It seemed more that the lift was swinging gently towards me, like an approaching pendulum. It was a pleasant sensation. Going towards it — or it approaching me — I felt this was the haven the tired and worried soul was desperate for.

They say the tireder you are the more are you likely to fall for the mechanised soporific. I was tired all right with the tensions of the day, but I had been in pain, too. My shoulder was giving a lot of it, and the right smack hitting the bars upside down had shaken my spine right through, up top and down bottom also.

The voice having been — I guessed — pushed off, and no further need to fight the bitter battle with the head, I was now swimming in the calm, warm waters of great relief.

It was as simple as that.

I think I fell into the lift and sat there up against the far wall. I think so because I didn't realise what I was doing for a while. Then I got up and punched the button.

The doors closed.

We went up, I suppose, because in a while we got there, but the important thing was that suddenly it was like being sprayed with an ice hose.

The weird peace dissipated.

The hypnotic sound was cut off by the closing doors.

The lift stopped. I felt the motion cease by that feeling the floor has started to sink. I stood there and thought a bit.

The hypnotic whispers would be outside again when I opened the doors. Tired and with many pains, I had been an easy victim. But that had been in the dark.

Standing there in the metal box I wondered if it would be the same in the light. I had to try it and see. The sweat broke out of my face at the thought of the fight.

For this time I was holding the button to keep the doors shut. Now I let it go and they slid back. I was outside the flats again and the bright evening sun shone through the vestibule windows.

I heard nothing at all.

Perhaps the hypnotic hiss was waiting,

having scared me once. I went into Sheila's flat and to the cigarette packet she had opened and left there. I ripped the filters off two and stuffed my ears with them.

Then I looked round.

There was no one in the flat. Kilgallen wasn't there, out or in any other state. As I went round from room to room I found myself gripping the handle of the machete in my belt. I must have been doing it all during the search.

There was a thud from somewhere. I was on the stairhead outside the flats when I heard it. It was rare to have a sound in that place, and I couldn't place where it came from.

I'd forgotten the fag ends in my ears then, and stood there straining to listen. Realising my fatheadedness I pulled the filters out, but instead of any solid sound I heard the coming and receding of the hypnotic hissing.

The filters went back quickly, but having heard the hiss, I kept thinking I could still hear it. It had bitten into me as far as that.

Suddenly a considerable rattling and thumping started up. With the things in my ears I had no chance to locate it but just chased through one flat after the other.

It was in the last flat, wriggling and twisting on the floor, kicking with one end against a built-in cupboard door.

It was somebody trussed up in a bedcover, head to foot, nothing showing.

'All right! Leave it!' I had to shout because when I touched the wriggling bundle it fought with even greater vigour.

It lay still enough for me to get the wrapper off, and there was Sheila, red in the face, eyes blazing with fury, gagged with a stocking and tied hand and foot with others.

I got her undone and she jumped up without thinking about cramp. As a result she stumbled and fell flat across the bed.

'Who did it?' I shouted.

'Kilgallen! He's crazed as a pot.' She rolled over on the bed and sat up. 'Great crunks!' she gasped and ran her fingers through her short, golden curls. 'He was like a lunatic.'

'Were you hurt?'

'I tried to play cool. I started trying to fight him off but it was useless. He smothered me. When I realised he wanted to tie me up, I thought, Let him. You can't be any worse off. So I did.'

I pulled the filters from my ears. I wasn't so frightened now somebody else was there with me. The hissing had stopped.

'Where did you go?' I said. 'Why did you run out of the gym?'

'Somebody slung a boomerang or something right over our heads from the passage,' she said. 'He turned round and then ran. So did I. It seemed like a chance to catch somebody — at last. I couldn't turn it down.'

'Did you see the man?'

'No. He was too far ahead for me. Kilgallen was some way ahead of me. He can run, that clopper. He turned up the stairs. I thought he'd seen the man go up them.'

'Did he say anything?'

'Yes. I heard him saying 'Henri! Henri!' As if he was saying it to himself and didn't know I was behind him.'

'Henri again!'

'Well, anyhow, he got up here and then he turned round and saw me. That did it. He went raving up the wall. I thought I was going to get my lot, so, like I said, I went along with it and hoped he would relent.'

'You must have been stacked in that cupboard.'

'I couldn't move for ages. Funny he's so good at tying people up. Most people who try don't know the first thing.'

'I'm glad you did get loose enough to kick up a din.'

'I nearly broke my neck. When you can't see, falling's like going headfirst down a coalmine.'

Then suddenly she put her hands over her face and started to cry. I sat alongside and put my arm round her, holding her tight. I didn't say anything. We had all three been screwed up like that and perhaps she was the only sensible one in letting go. She clung to me and shook heavily with her sobbing and laughing and trying to stop doing either.

Holding her there gave me some purpose in going on to the end with this thing and thinking of winning it. Not losing it, as I had lately been getting into the idea of. Because just hoping to exist in the face of all is losing as near as makes no difference.

She calmed down very suddenly and I kissed her.

'We can't just sit here,' she said, and got up.

'Where do you operate the Tannoy?'

'In a downstairs office. Have you heard anything?'

'A lot. Let's go down.'

Then she stopped, calm reason fully returned.

'You didn't get out, then.'

'No.' I said. 'There were reasons. I had to come back in. I haven't seen Kilgallen since he was with you.'

'What's that you've got?' she said. seeing me fingering the handle of he machete.

'I hope it will be a boomerang,' I said. 'Come on, down.'

We went downstairs. The sun was low,

slanting in at the windows so you screwed your eyes to look out that side. Half-way down I touched her arm and ran back up.

The lift doors were shut. More of the doors game.

'What's the matter?' she called and ran up again.

Like me she wasn't keen to be alone any more.

'Somebody's been at the lift since I came. I left it open, but I'm so used to the door game now all I want to do is catch some clever bird inside it.'

I pressed the button. The indicators still weren't working. They were on the house circuits and the lift on its own separate link which the operators, for obvious reasons, hadn't turned off.

The doors slid aside. She was holding my arm and got it tighter when the doors opened from reaction.

Which meant that Kilgallen just came at me from out of the lift with almost nothing but a bad shoulder to put up against him.

9

Big and ugly in fury, Kilgallen rushed out of that lift like a human bull. With Sheila on my left arm, and my right shoulder burning with pain, I didn't much like the impending combat.

Sheila spent less time thinking about it. She pulled my arm sharply, swinging me round sideways towards the lift. Kilgallen's aim was shifted. He half-turned but almost lost his balance.

She let me go and I got hold of his big, flailing arm as it went by me and tipped him headlong on to a chesterfield. Then I went and got his arm behind and held him there.

'Cut the humour, Kilgallen,' I said. 'Just relax. I want to talk to you, so get the steam out of your head.'

He just laid there, face down, letting the latest hypnotic instructions fade out of his bemused brain.

She came up and watched.

'It's him. It must be,' she said.

'We should be near finding out,' I said. 'Now the hypnotic hiss is rumbled we can get in between it and him. Even if it means bunging his ears up.'

'That explains the long ride in the car coming here,' she said. 'If he's innocent.'

'Yes. I seem to remember him saying the radio was on. In any case, it wouldn't have had to be pushing out any programme. Just the mush, changing frequency in that quiet, regular way would do the trick. Consciously, you wouldn't even notice it if you were doing something else.'

Kilgallen didn't seem to hear anything of what we said but was quite still. I kept on looking round at the open lift to make sure it hadn't done another of its vanishing tricks.

'Okay. Let up,' Kilgallen said.

He sounded tired, all emotion spent. I got off him and he just lay there a little longer, then finally got up into a sitting position.

'Where did you go?' I said. 'Just before you came up in that lift?'

'I don't know where it was. It was bloody dark.'

'The cellars,' I said, and turned to Sheila. 'What's down there?'

'Some offices which we don't use, and a couple of strong rooms. The offices are meant for when we expand. That is, if we ever recover from this jaunt, which I'm beginning to doubt.'

'So it's all just a filing store?'

'Armoured. But yes, just that.'

'There was a lot of talking,' Kilgallen said. 'I couldn't understand it. I really think I must be going mad. I heard the words but I couldn't understand the sense. I kept trying. It was like trying to catch snowflakes going by.'

'You're not mad,' I said. 'We have definite proof of that now.' I told him about the hypnotic trick.

He shook his head.

'I don't remember anything unusual like that,' he said.

'The whole point is it isn't unusual. It's just like a background mush on radio reception. The point about your sanity is that nobody would go to great risk and expense to prove you mad if you were gone already.'

He laughed and shook his head.

'That's an argument, I suppose,' he said. 'I'm not really receptive to such logic just now.'

'It'll come to you gradually. There won't be any more fits. We've got the measure of that one. I want to know about Liston. The treatment first was a long sleep, you said.'

'Drugs. Yes. Three days I think it was. One doesn't actually know. You have to go by the calendar.'

'Did you have any treatment by hypnosis?'

'Yes. There was a young doctor called Landau. I think it was more of a test than a treatment. The idea was that it might help in teaching me to fight these tensions.'

'But you couldn't?'

'With my involvements, how could I? There's always something.'

'Why were you linking with Henri Marc?'

'Blind landing. A — ' Then he realised.

'What do secrets matter now? If you don't come out with the lot, you'll be going into jug with the lot unsaid. It won't pay you. Well, blind landing for aircraft. A new system perhaps?'

'Yes. In development stage. I know the Americans are after it. They get after everything, even if it's only to kill it.'

'It wouldn't be that in this case?'

'No. The idea here seems to be to kill me.' He was very bitter then. 'If what you say is true, then I killed that girl while under a hypnotic influence.'

'I think the influence was to make you believe you had killed her.'

'But I did speak with her, you know, and the photographs — '

'And the brief-case. Somebody took that. It wasn't the girl. She was dead then.'

'You don't suggest I was hypnotised into not seeing a third person there?' He was heavily sarcastic.

'With the shock of finding you had shot her dead, you wouldn't have noticed much that was going on around you.'

'But you came in immediately after. No one passed you going out.'

'There is a back door,' I said. 'An intruder could have got out that way and locked it from the outside.'

'How did nobody think of that before?' Sheila said, surprised.

'That way couldn't have been used after I got shut in here. I wasn't having my brain buzzed. I heard everything that happened, specially every time a lock clicked, up to the last, when there was too much noise just at the instant. Obviously that moment was chosen when noise covered the click. But from the back door and on the outside, one couldn't hear what went on inside.'

'You sound more confident,' Sheila said.

'I'm building up,' I said. 'I think now that one man involved is an architect's assistant. His firm built this place and did the alterations at Liston. I was at Liston during the time you, Kilgallen, were there. For all I know you were asleep at the time. But there is the connection between you and me. After all, the common factor between us isn't money, but something we both know about Liston which we can't value.'

'Landau?'

'That would be too obvious, too open altogether. It's more likely someone who didn't seem directly connected with your treatment, but who knew exactly what your reactions to it were. Can you think who that might be?'

'Any one of the staff, I suppose.'

'And Lady Kilgallen,' said Sheila suddenly.

Kilgallen glared at her.

'What the devil do you mean?' he said.

'What I say. She could have known. One mustn't leave out possibilities, however unpleasant they are.'

'I refuse to discuss my wife!'

'But she may be the key, an innocent key,' I said. 'We have to think of that.'

'We had parted before that breakdown. She could have had nothing whatever to do with Liston.'

'How do you know she didn't call there?' I said. 'You were unconscious for three solid days. Anyone could have come in that time and you would not have known.'

'Impossible!'

'But your parting wasn't firm at that time,' I said. 'You told me that she went to Perpignan in order to think things over. That shows her considerable doubt. Sometime after, you had the breakdown. She might well have repented and come to see you.'

He laughed with a wild bitterness.

'And then — ?' he shouted.

'And then she was persuaded against trying to make things up and came no more,' I said. 'That fits with the picture you have painted of a wife who really didn't want to go at the start. It would be a natural thing for a woman in such a position to come back when she heard of the illness.'

'If she came, I was never told.'

'She could have made the request you weren't told, specially if she realised she was only making things worse.'

He dropped his head into his hands as he sat there, and for a while he was quite still.

'It could be right,' he said at last.

'Soon after she remarried,' I said. 'So that this man Blackhurst would have been told every detail that was known to her. There is your key.'

'I wouldn't put anything past that bastard,' he said sourly. 'But he hasn't the guts to organise anything like this.'

'He was here,' I reminded him.

'He wouldn't do it. He lives by asking for money. He wouldn't risk anything by way of work or planning a thing like this. Organisation takes a lot of work and application. He hasn't anything of that quality about him.'

'He could provide information for others who have such application. Another firm who wants your landing gear.'

'Why involve Henri?'

'When did you last see Henri? Think hard.'

'This afternoon.'

'Or somebody you thought was he.'

We both watched him trying to be sure of what he had seen.

'You called after him, remember,' I

said. 'So he must have been running away from you. You just saw a man's back that looked like Henri's. A hyp suggestion made you certain it was Henri. Possible?'

'Possible, yes. I can't be sure.'

'Henri is in trouble in your villa at Perpignan,' I said. 'He, like you, is a wealthy manufacturer. Now, here is a queer coincidence. He is in trouble there, with the cops all round the place. You get fixed here with what must end in having cops all round your place. In fact, you could both have been framed at the same time.'

'I hadn't looked at it that way!'

'No, but now you do, there's a possibility that we shouldn't look for plain industrial spies,' I said. 'I think we should consider the possibility that an international bunch are in this for the money. Spies don't get much from Governments. They could double up by working for industry. But the fixing of you and Henri reveals strongarm methods I don't think industry would go for. Suppose we have a gang of Frenchies, with Blackhurst the lingual link?'

He got up and started to walk.

'It is possible. Yes. It's more possible than what we have been thinking of. I have refused to believe that any colleagues of mine could be involved in such a murderous business. But if this is organised by outsiders — yes. Then it all becomes possible.'

'It changes things,' Sheila said.

'It means if we start to win — that seems a long shot but it could happen — then we'll be up against wholesale murderers. We'd better not forget that. We haven't got a weapon beyond this old broad blade.'

I wagged the machete at them.

'They must be in the building?' Sheila said.

'Somebody must,' I said. 'We ought to search the cellar rooms but there's no light down there, nor anywhere else, for that matter. Only down there, you have to have something. We haven't, have we?'

'There are lanterns, but down in the locked cupboards,' the girl said.

'We've got to go down,' I said. 'Somehow or other we've also got to see what we're doing.'

'Jane's handbag!' Sheila said, and ran.

When she came back, it was not just with a torch, but with the bag.

'There's a transmission on,' she said quickly. 'Listen!'

A voice was speaking quickly.

'You'll have to come in,' it said. 'We can't deal with the three of them. They're not scared like you thought. They're mad as hell about everything. You've got to come in and do this yourself. Out.'

We listened, but there was no reply.

'Do you read me?' the voice said again. 'We can't deal with the three of 'em. You must come in. Out.'

After a while a voice answered, rather fainter from distance.

'Do you want the police in? Out.'

'For God's sake, no! That original plan isn't going to work. I can't tell you more. You must come in and deal with them. Out.'

'It's got to work. That Perpignan one's working fine. They've got him on murder as planned. The other part must fit in. Out.'

'You don't get the drift. We can't handle it. The original plan can't work. The Blake bastard has jammed it. You'll have to come in. Out.'

'Okay then. Plan two. But I can't be there before nine. The alibi depends on it. Ends.'

★　★　★

I think we all looked at our watches at the same moment.

'Seven fifty-eight,' Kilgallen said, and he grinned briefly. 'I'm sorry to hear you called a bastard, but I'm very pleased they consider me sane. Was there a torch in the bag?'

'Yes. A good light spreader. You can focus these to a pinpoint for burglary or spread them out to light up airfields for moths.' Sheila giggled a little.

'It's surprising how bad news can cheer people up,' I said. 'Your minds, like memory, just play on the green bits. We've ruined their plan one, somehow, so you cheer. But you mustn't ignore plan two, which obviously includes doing in the three of us.'

'But we've got till nine to find the others,' Sheila said.

'Let us also bear in mind they are probably hearing everything we say, which is a big disadvantage,' I reminded them.

'But they have already admitted defeat in our hearing,' said Kilgallen. 'So they cannot be greatly comforted. In fact, having threatened to go into the basement, I'll bet they've evacuated it.'

'It's a hope,' I said. 'I hate trying to fight by pocket flashlight.'

Then we turned and looked at the lift. It was still there, wide open.

'Is there a way out of the cellars other than that?' I said.

'Not that I know of,' Sheila said.

'Try the light,' I said.

The torch worked all right. We went into the lift.

'When we land,' I said, 'the man goes two paces to the left of the lift. The girl goes three the other way. I go out alone. Wait till you see the light. Just stand still until then.'

I pushed the button and snapped out the lift light. We stood in complete darkness with only the very faint whine of the mechanism to tell us we moved. Then that clicked off and we just heard the doors sliding apart.

I stepped out and went ahead until I felt the wall with my fingers. Then I turned along it to the right. It was as dark as The Pit.

When I stopped by the office door I listened. I couldn't hear anything except a soft mush from the Tannoy. The speaker must have been over my head somewhere.

As I heard it a slow panic spread. If they started that hypnotic trick while we were all in the dark, we couldn't be sure it wouldn't start to work. We were all tensed, waiting, listening; just the correct conditions for a background suggestion theme to get like a worm into the brain.

That idea alone was bad. Instead of listening for any movement, I found myself listening only to the faint hiss, trying to make out if the undulation of the tone was beginning.

What made it worse was the absolute

blackness. That made it possible to feel that you were floating in space, or standing upside down, anything. I kept pressing my feet down hard to remind my brain I was still upright.

Yet I didn't dare use the torch before I had some idea where everybody was. To use it suddenly then would have meant blinding ourselves as well as anybody else.

I got my handkerchief and bound it over the torch lens. That would ease the initial blast of light when I finally did turn it on.

I tore myself from listening to that hiss. I was making it get me when it was doing nothing but stay ready for a transmission that apparently nobody wanted to make.

The door was unlocked when I tried it. Inside it was as black as out. I shone the masked torch for an instant. There was an office with sheeted furniture like ghosts standing about. It looked chilly, frightening. I don't like hooded things. You don't know what's underneath besides the chair.

I went round, flinging the sheets up off the chairs. They were empty. I felt a great gust of relief at that and after a brief look round the room with the dull yellow light I went back to the door.

It was shut.

A sudden panicky thought struck me as I fumbled for the handle. Was this the final sordid door joke? If so, what silent one was creeping around?

The door was locked when I tried it, but it must have been by a bolt for I had heard no click of wards.

Backing away from it I shone the torch round the walls again. There was another door, probably leading into the next office. It was unlocked and I went through and shone the light on another collection of sheeted chairs. But these looked different. Very different. They had heads under the sheets. Sideways bent heads, like heads on broken necks. A pair of legs stuck out from under one sheet.

And then, as I watched in a kind of cold horror that kept me quite still, I saw a slight movement from under one of the sheets.

It was very slight, but it was enough.

I backed out through the door quickly. Not for me that kind of a trap.

And then I heard the noise from somewhere above me. The soft, steady coming and going of the hypnotic mush.

10

I stood in darkness for a moment, letting the weirdie sound come and recede in my brain. It was soothing. It made it begin to seem that nothing mattered. That you could let go and be asleep and at peace.

While somebody came in and cut your throat.

The only thing to shake that hypnotic influence was action. The only action I had there was to challenge the people hiding under those sheets. Better to try and fight two or even three of them with my little knife than to let go and fall half-daft so that they could come in at their leisure.

I went back to that door and shone the light on the chair shapes — the chairs with heads.

There was a faint sign of movement, but not much. They were holding still.

I went to the nearest and whipped the sheet up and over.

There was a man, his head on his chest, fast asleep.

For a few seconds I just stood there looking at him. It must be Marsh. Marsh, fast asleep. Marsh out to the wide many hours after he had been made to disappear.

His pulse was steady but very slow. I went to the other sheeted figures and uncovered two girls, a redhead and a blonde. Jane Shore, who had left the bag behind, and Mary Adur who had rushed out of an already untidy flat so fast she hadn't taken anything.

No, I had that wrong. One of them had been drinking a lager in the bar. As Mary was in a dressing gown flopping there in the chair I guessed the drinker had been Jane.

All out. Hours out. How the hell was that done? How had it been done in the original capture?

Drugs, obviously, but people like these three wouldn't sit still and let somebody come up on them with a needle.

Drugs in their drinks? But only Marsh and Jane had had drinks. There was no sign of any such thing in Mary's flat. She had just come rushing out.

These problems, coming in fast, pushed the hissing of the loudspeaker back in my mind.

I got Marsh's wrists and made a quick examination. No sign of a needle.

But on the back of his right hand there was a small pinpoint of blood. Ideas began to come in.

I turned the light on the girl in the dressing gown. Her hands had no puncture visible, but in the vee of the neck of the gown there was another pinpoint of blood on the clear white flesh.

The redhead Jane was not so obvious. I couldn't find a pinprick until I thought of her sitting at the bar, her back towards the doors. I flopped her forward in the chair and looked at the back of her neck. There was a pinpoint of blood.

So now the play was getting somewhere. All three had been laid out, taken by surprise obviously by somebody they hadn't seen, or they would have dodged the jabs.

Then how?

A connecting link with Kilgallen came in. His treatment had had him laid out for days with drugs. Here were three active people laid out for ten hours plus.

Again there was the trace back to the nursing home.

But how to get the needle into three active, suspicious people trained in the art of avoiding trouble and surprise? Such a trick seemed impossible, but it was the simplest dodge of them all, as it turned out. The impossible was as easy as dammit.

Suddenly I heard someone speak; shortly, cursing.

I snapped out the light, turned to the open doorway and grabbed the handle of the huge knife in my belt. But nothing happened and the systematic coming and going of the mush ended abruptly.

The Tannoy had been switched off. The swearing had come from it. One man had cursed another, that had been the answer.

Flipping the light on again I ran out through the next office and banged on the door.

'Kilgallen! Open the door here!'

There was a pause, then I heard Sheila.

'Feel along the wall. Here. It's along here.'

'I'll keep knocking,' I said.

'Okay. Knock on,' I heard Kilgallen say breathlessly.

He came to the door. I heard his hands pawing across the plain panel, and fumbled around.

'Got it!' he said. 'It's a flush bolt. Hang on!'

I heard nothing of the bolt slip back. The door opened. I shone the light down so as not to blind them.

'They're in the next office,' I said. 'Your mob, Sheila. Fast asleep. No harm done. Leave it now. They're upstairs after all. The Tannoy room.'

'They can't be,' she said. 'I looked there. The door's open. You can see right in. There was nobody.'

'Then they may have a tap on it somewhere else in the line,' I said, and shone the beam to the lift. 'Come on up!'

I shoved her towards the lift, Kilgallen following.

'Are you sure they're all right?' she said, resisting.

'Yes, but they won't be if you don't do as you're told. Get in the lift!'

She stopped pushing against me and almost tumbled into the box.

As the doors slid open to the ground floor corridor it was as before, wide, empty, silent. I steered them away down to the gym. They were both surprised, but once in there I slipped the open doors so that they swung to.

'They'll get away!' Sheila said angrily.

'They can't. They're waiting for their boss. They can't go till we're fixed. You heard it all. Now hear something else. I think this is the only spot in the building that isn't bugged.'

I told them about the three downstairs.

'Impossible!' Sheila burst out. 'You couldn't have got them all by surprise!'

'There's no other way,' I said. 'You've got the nursing home technique running through this from the start. The long-term sleep drug, and the hypnotic effects all based on the reaction of Lord Kilgallen in the home.

'The hypnosis is an electronic device, very easily made in your own plant, or anybody else's once the trick is known. So the line reads nursing home to your office, and then a connecting agent to the French side.

'Blackhurst. It must be Blackhurst, whatever you say. You say he hasn't the drive. But he could be pushed. That sort of man has weaknesses all along. Anyone of importance could be used as a blackmail pusher. That would encourage him on.

'You've been far too keen on showing his lack of strength. The reason for that is your wish to keep your ex-wife out of trouble. But it's too late for that. She was in it from the start.'

'I won't listen — !'

He started off with a roar, but Sheila cut him short.

'Don't let prejudice get in the way,' she snapped. 'Who else but a woman who lived with you could have known all the tiny details that had to be known to be used against your sanity? Who else? Nobody. Nobody in the wide world could have known as much about you. Even the nursing home could only go by hearsay, and what she could tell them. That's why she went there. Not to see you, but to help them treat you. That must be the truth of it.'

He stood there, fists clenched, breathing hard.

'After all,' Sheila said, 'she did leave you for this other man. You didn't leave her.'

'I refuse — '

'How did you pay her?' I said. 'Did the amounts vary?'

'There were occasional extra requests. Trouble with that bastard. He was always running into serious debt, and of course, that let her in, too.'

'So you paid up as required?'

'What would you have done?'

'Left it entirely to lawyers.'

Then he went saggy and shrugged.

'That's what I did in the end.'

'But a certain alimony continued?' I said.

'It did. I gave her the divorce, you remember.'

'Adultery?' Sheila said quickly.

'Yes. I hired a girl. I thought at the time it was a distasteful thing to do but — ' he gave a short laugh. 'She was quite a girl. We stayed a week so that there would be no mistake. It rather eased the pangs. One is human on occasion.'

'Did you see the girl afterwards?' Sheila said suddenly.

'Yes. I have seen her on occasion.'

'The divorce was undefended?'

'Of course. Very little publicity, thank heaven.'

'But it didn't affect your position with the organisation?' I said.

'It did,' he said. 'Things were very awkward for a long while. It was partly the anxiety over that that caused the breakdown.'

'So that would have given the idea of the faked photos,' I said. 'A second scandal would have finished you?'

'I think so.'

'Yes. It's what you would think that matters here. It had to be the motive for the shooting of the model. The whole plan against you was based on things that

224

had actually happened to you before and to which your reactions were known. It comes closer to your wife all the time, doesn't it?'

He started to break.

'I don't know.'

'She knew Blackhurst while she was still married to you? That's the truth of it, not that she was neglected but that she had another man?'

'He got in. He was the type!'

'That doesn't alter what I said. She moved out on you while still married. She goes off with a ladies' man who picks them up, as you say, like daisies by the way. She was easy with him. Do you really think that two such morally dishonest people have stayed together? Wouldn't it be more likely they didn't stick together at all, except for gathering money from easy taps?'

He just stared then, but from his face the truth was plain.

'I don't know,' he muttered.

'Henri Marc is held by the police,' I said. 'We know that. What reason? He's too rich to steal anything. What would be the popular conception of a rich Frenchman's murder be? The murder of his mistress. Marc has no wife.'

'I don't know. This is all guesswork!'

'The mistress was your wife,' I said. 'You knew that. All your jealousy was reserved for Henri Marc. It was he you kept thinking you saw. He who was on your mind all the time. Not Blackhurst, the flower picker, but Marc, the old trusted colleague and friend. That is the man you kept chasing. When Blackhurst showed up here, you ran away from him. You didn't want him to see you. If you'd met he might have said, 'How's our ex-wife?' That was the reason you hid, wasn't it?'

He didn't reply.

'The letter you had from Perpignan, warning you not to go or phone there, was not from the agents as such, but from agents who had been working as your private eyes. That so? Keeping a watch on the villa and your wife and Henri Marc.'

He walked away some paces then turned back.

'I still love her,' he said. 'I have never

tried to hide that.'

'What you really mean is that you still regarded her as your property, despite everything that had happened. You are, after all, Lord Kilgallen, self-made. To be the king of everything except your wife is a galling situation.'

His fists clenched and unclenched but he said nothing.

'Suppose we look at this from a different standpoint,' I said. 'Suppose we say that there is a degree of instability in you, a tendency to savage retaliation, and rigid pride. The Othello trend. Supposing that you organised your wife's death and the conviction of Marc for murder way over in your house at Perpignan?'

'You are the madman now!' he shouted.

'The people one hires for such trade are not the most reliable or loyal of employees. If they can get so much money from you for the job, they may be let in close enough to see that more money still can be made.

'To involve your wife in the murder they would have to know about her, perhaps to know her. She has been milking your account with success for a long time, then suddenly you cut that source short by handing over the reins to your lawyers.

'Surely she looks for another source? You wouldn't know if she has been using your money to buy up shares in your companies. It would be done behind some holding name.

'If this plot against you succeeds, what happens to the share market? Tremendous losses. Downward dip. Originator of the whole organisation finished, out.

'She buys more. Rock bottom price. Where does she get the money? Henri Marc. Up goes the price again because why? Because Marc has rushed in and saved the organisation, and is now in control.

'So Kilgallen is away in the jug and everything he has is gone. Marc and your wife are kings of your castle.

'Your employees get to know all this proposal because they are watching your wife. What better then to increase their investment, and to keep to your plot of getting rid of Marc and your ex-wife and themselves getting in on the share racket?'

'I know nothing! Nothing!' he said.

'The murder is accomplished. Marc is arrested. The gendarmes are in control. They dig up some indication of the share racket and contact your office yesterday.

'You are shaken by this. Badly shaken, because to you it means someone in the office is double crossing you. And that is the reason you rang LOHM to make this appointment. You wanted to find who the double-crosser was.

'But your call never got here. It was tapped in your own office and the appointment made there. Then the crossers came here, prepared the stage and fixed you.

'Look, Kilgallen. You are finished all ways, whichever way you look at it. Your shares are down and your chair is empty. Someone can make a fortune from the dip, and gain control. Someone well trusted in your organisation. Someone who has been with you for years, knew your wife, knew everything about you, except perhaps the most intimate details which, as Sheila said, only a wife would know.'

'She wouldn't!' he roared out suddenly. 'The most faithful, loyal servant — '

'Not all secretaries are in love with their masters,' I said. 'Some secretaries, being regarded as dispensable chattels by their masters, are easy flowers for daisy pickers.'

I leaned against the wall wondering why he didn't go for me again. But he didn't. He stood there snorting like a bull and staring at the ground as if trying to see how much of his life lay in pieces there.

★ ★ ★

It was then eight forty-three.

'Who will come?' Sheila said. 'A woman?'

'I don't think she'll come. That wouldn't work out right at all, would it?'

I looked up at the cut end of the rope under the steel beam.

'Do you remember any coloured men on the staff at Liston Grange?' I asked.

230

Kilgallen looked up then.

'There were a couple of trainee nurses,' he said. 'Sterilising needles. Pushing the pram round — '

For the moment he had given up. I had got him with the truth, it seemed. Whatever the rig of the girl murder had against him, it was clear then that the rig in the villa at Perpignan had been his. I don't know French law, but I assume if you murder someone on the Spanish border from a comfortable chairman's seat in Lonon they can get you for it. I think he knew.

'So it'll be the hired thugs,' Sheila said. 'Can't we wake the others up?'

'The Big Cheese wouldn't have said nine if he'd thought they could be shaken awake,' I said. 'They can't be due up yet.'

I went out and along the corridor to the double glass doors. The sun shadows were long out on the grass. I went back and into the bar.

He must have come to his senses at some time for she was covered up again with a silk cover from the grand piano. I got myself a drink and went out into the corridor.

Kilgallen was walking slowly along towards me, his hands in his pockets, brooding. We had both been right, Sheila and I. She had said he was guilty, I'd said innocent. Both right. Different murders.

Sheila was behind him. I took my glass and went through the offices. Nobody there. Like all the rest of the time, they were running ahead of us.

And then I remembered the closing of that door of the flat upstairs just when I'd pulled Sheila in.

I hadn't seen anybody shut that door. Certainly there had been no one outside, so it must have been inside, and not a hand at eye level, but probably a foot shoving it hard.

Kilgallen's foot.

I had been making mysteries for myself. He had been hypped into doing things they wanted. This was just one more action upon instructions.

But no sound. No spoken word. I didn't remember even the mushing of the Tannoy at that time.

And then I went out into the corridor and chased him up. Sheila came up behind me, scared to leave me, I hope.

'Kilgallen,' I said, 'there's time to open this out. It could help before we all get sewn up. After all, you'd be better off doing twenty years than dead tonight. It's never nice to think of being dead in a minute. There's a kind of curtain starts closing over, smothering. Suddenly you realise how fine it is to breathe, and you want to go on doing it. After all, life has many degrees. Even in a prison these days, things are very easy for those who haven't been in the crime business all their lives — '

'I'm concerned with the French law, not ours,' he snapped back.

We stopped by the glass doors.

'I'd forgotten the knife,' I said. 'But are you sure they could get near enough to use it?'

'If they can get as close as you, they will,' he said. He leaned up against the bar doorway. 'Let's drink. I may not have to worry about the French.'

'Okay. Let's drink. Sheila. Please

dispense.' I gave her my emptied glass as she went by. 'Kilgallen, where are the men in this house?'

'I don't know any more than you. But I'm sure your theory that they hear us and move ahead of us is right.'

I shoved him into the bar lounge, unfixed the doors and let them swing shut.

'There are too many open doors around,' I said. 'A closed one makes a man do something, even if only create a small draught. Now I have a little more to say.

'Three people are downstairs, knocked out by hypo jabs. How? The only way I can think of is the way they knock out wild animals when they want to treat them.

'They fire hypo darts from rifles. The dart sticks in, lays the animal out, everybody walks in, do what they want, go. The animal comes to, is better.'

'A soft shot would have been heard,' said Sheila, fetching the drinks.

'Not a blowpipe,' I said. 'Now if you look down on the walls of your favourite local pub, Sheila, you'll see spears, shields, arrows and blowpipes. If you are a gentleman of very quiet habits and you are a man who has used such pipes before, even if only in practice, you can open a door a little, have the pipe ready, puff and the dart be in the skin before the recipient knows anything has happened.'

'Heavens!' she said. 'I didn't think of that! And Jane on the barstool here — easy. And Mary, running out on some sort of alarm — All dead easy and not a sound to warn anybody. You're a genius.'

'Somebody else was one before me. So now we have a very quick, light and silent-footed gent, probably barefooted, who can use the peashooter technique with darts. He can also sling a knife. You also have someone who knew what knockout drops Kilgallen had in the hosp. Well, so what? It's all unusually unEnglish, who are very heavy-footed and noisy, having little to fear but the taxman.

'Aid this quick and gifted gentleman with another who knows every twist, turn and trick of the building, because he helped design it, and you have an advantage even over someone who lives here.

'Every bolt, every lock oiled to soundlessness before we get here. Everything laid out for them against us. Okay, we play you draughts, but you'll be blinded because we shall make sure somebody will keep making you look behind you as we move our pieces.'

It was eight-fifty.

Sheila saw me look at a clock behind the bar.

'What are you going to do?' she said urgently.

'Up to now it's been us wondering what they will do,' I said. 'That's put us at a disadvantage all along. Now let them wonder what we will do.'

I went behind the bar with her.

'You should have soda in that Scotch, Kilgallen,' I said. 'It penetrates the stomach walls so much quicker.'

I bent down and started on a soda crate which I had seen there before. I lifted out the siphons one by one and landed them quietly on the counter towels, those thick things they spread out because the modern way of serving beer is so dirty. I put up eight squirters.

'If they can't see, there is always a moment of advantage,' I said. 'So far it's all been hearing. Come on, K. Fill it up.'

I squirted his glass full. It hissed out like an old train. Any mike in that wall must have got it.

Several times it seemed that the clock had stopped, it was so slow. I walked all round the walls of that room, making myself acquainted with everything to the detail degree and when I came back to the bar I lifted the phone.

It tinged.

For a moment I don't think any one of us realised what that meant, the shock, after the long silent day was so great. Then it seemed we all dived for it, and almost fell on each other like a scrum.

'By God, it's on!' I said and went to dial.

A voice from the earhole said, 'Mr. Blake? I think I recognise the voice.'

'Who is it?'

'If you will look out of the window for the next minute or two you will see for yourself. It will be a surprise, I promise.'

He rang off and immediately the thing went dead again.

I could think of no reason for that call except that it was to make me look out the front while somebody came up at the back.

Conversely it could have been to make me think that and then come up the front way. Obviously I was then very tired.

When I told what had been said, Kilgallen just stared rudely and turned away. Sheila laughed a bit.

'It's needling still,' she said.

'Why don't you open out, K?' I said. 'What's the good of holding it now? In five minutes we may all get blown to hell. They've got to do something about us, haven't they?'

He turned back.

'So far as I know, everything you said is right but one. It was agreed that the letter from Perpignan should be sent here, before I made the appointment yesterday. If the scheme was successful, that is. In other words, I decided on LOHM some days ago. I told my secretary that, too, when she suggested that firm.'

'Tell me one thing,' I said. 'If you get away out of here now, what will you do?'

'There surely is only one thing I can do,' he said, showing his teeth. 'Find my bloody secretary!'

'Perhaps you will,' I said. 'Blackhurst is coming up the drive now. He doesn't give in easily, does he?'

We watched him come up to the steps. He walked quite slowly, enjoying the evening. More than anything even that strange day, this looked like something out of a dream.

I went to the doors and out. He came up the steps and prodded the bellpush again. Nothing happened.

Then he turned and walked away. I could almost hear him humming a pleasant tune, he was so relaxed.

The explosion went off down the passage behind me. It was more a fire bomb than a high explosive, but the bang of the air travelling fast in rapid expansion laid me on my face on the floor.

Looking back from the flat down position it looked as if there was a lane of fire stretching right down the corridor roaring as it tried to get a hold. It seemed to be belching from the lift doorway.

Sheila appeared at the lounge doors then went back again. I saw Kilgallen's big shadow near her. Then I saw two men come out of the junction at the bottom of the corridor where the locked cupboards were.

They ran across and were heading for the side door to the garden.

I got up and ran too. There was one thing I knew which they had forgotten in the panic of being double-crossed.

In such a place where every precaution had been taken in its design, there would be fire sprinklers that would drench any fire that started.

As I ran down along the far wall from the fire, they started. It was like the biggest thunderstorm in creation.

Sheila came out behind me, following. The two men came back into sight and dodged into the gym. The fire was changing into steam as we ran through the streaming wet.

But it was good at last to see the

enemy. Everything seemed suddenly quite sane and in good order.

When we got into the gym, the two wretches had got the far escape door open and I saw the last, a small, black-faced man, lithe as a boy, slip out like an eel into the evening sun.

We got out there into the bushes of the fruit gardens and stopped. Everything was still again.

We searched as far as we could, then ran for the drive, which, of course, was quite empty. From all we saw there need never have been anybody there at all. Just like the rest of the day.

I looked at her, and suddenly she laughed. She was dripping, as I was, and her dress was plastered against her body so that I could see every splendid line. Her golden hair stuck to her face like string.

'Well, that's it, I suppose,' I said. And then I remembered Kilgallen.

We ran back and we went into the streaming corridor and we looked every-where and shouted for him, but we knew the answer.

'Better get some police, I suppose,' she said.

'Yes,' I said. 'After all, what comes next is nothing to do with us. Pass it on.'

I left Sheila to her companions and let them find the police. I drove into London and to Kilgallen's offices where a commissionaire was on weekend duty. He let me go up. Kilgallen was there, rough, dirty, hot and tired.

'Can't trace her anywhere,' he said gruffly. 'Left her flat, the porter said. Very methodical. Gave up the key, too.'

'Well, that's what you wanted, isn't it? Proof she was in it?'

'No,' he said glumly. 'I wanted proof she wasn't.' Then he looked at me and shrugged. 'I'm just a dead loss with women. Don't seem to know a damn thing of what they think or do. Just when I think they're doing one thing, they're round the back of me, laughing. I'd better give 'em up.'

'What about yourself? Will you give yourself up?'

'I'll wait till the gendarmes ask for me,' he said, and sat down at his empty, weekend desk. 'Might get a bit of work done in between.'

True to character. First things first. Concentrate on work. Don't see a damn thing that's going on all round you.

I said good-bye, but he was already at work on papers from his desk drawer.

This was Saturday night, so no use trying to contact the architects until Monday morning. By then, I was sure, they would find themselves an assistant short.

So I went to the one place I knew I would find a contact, to my old club, whose last week was ending. Jamie, gloomy despite a Scotch on his desk, was in the act of packing up.

'Thanks for putting me on to LOHM,' I said.

'You fixed up all right? Good. I never heard of them, but I was assured they were dead with it.'

'They're with it, and almost dead, too,' I said. 'There was a fire bomb connected to a bell push by a coloured mental nurse. They forgot the sprinklers.'

'Sounds mental to me,' he said, staring.

'I'll tell you about it,' I said, and did.

'Struth!' he said, gaping. 'But the fellow who recommended them was a business consultant who offered to help us out of our financial troubles, but even he saw it was no good.'

'By the name of Blackhurst.'

'Yes.'

'I think he's run off with Kilgallen's secretary. He's been successful with women till now. But it's possible he might find her more than a match for him, if she engineered all this.'

'But you know, I mentioned you,' said Jamie, frowning, 'and I said about shooting and it was he suggested LOHM. So I told you. But it almost seems as if — '

'As if he meant to get me down there and have Kilgallen kill me as well as the bird,' I said.

'Yes. What for?'

'I have made enemies in the past,' I said. 'One never knows where they get to, now that it's comparatively easy to get out of prison. In any case, as the great Christy said, 'The more the merrier'. He hoped to prove his insanity by sheer weight of murders. If Kilgallen could be shown to have done two, he'd be well on the way and the business passed into the hands of the secretary, who now, owing to a failure in the plans, has had to vanish.'

He gave me a cigarette and I said, 'Why did you have the girl killed, Jamie?'

He turned away.

'She was a blackmailer. If you wanted to know why the club had to finish, you should have asked her.'

'She was shot dead when I found her. They had a coloured nurse who seemed expert at shooting, knife throwing and blowpipe darting.'

He turned round.

'Kilgallen didn't kill her?'

'No. He was hypnotised into thinking he did. I told you.'

'Yes. I suppose I was a bit too emotional to notice exactly what you said.'

'Pity you got mixed up, Jamie,' I said. 'I liked the club. It was, at any rate, comparatively safe.'

We do hope that you have enjoyed reading this large print book.

Did you know that all of our titles are available for purchase?

We publish a wide range of high quality large print books including:
Romances, Mysteries, Classics
General Fiction
Non Fiction and Westerns

Special interest titles available in large print are:
The Little Oxford Dictionary
Music Book, Song Book
Hymn Book, Service Book

Also available from us courtesy of Oxford University Press:
Young Readers' Dictionary
(large print edition)
Young Readers' Thesaurus
(large print edition)

For further information or a free brochure, please contact us at:
Ulverscroft Large Print Books Ltd.,
The Green, Bradgate Road, Anstey,
Leicester, LE7 7FU, England.
Tel: (00 44) **0116 236 4325**
Fax: (00 44) **0116 234 0205**

Other titles in the
Linford Mystery Library:

DEATH SQUAD

Basil Copper

Lost in a fog on National Forest terrain, Mike Faraday, the laconic L.A. private investigator, hears shots. A dying man staggers out of the bushes. Paul Dorn, a brilliant criminal lawyer, is quite dead when Mike gets to him. So how could he be killed again in a police shoot-out in L.A. the same night? The terrifying mystery into which Faraday is plunged convinces him that a police death squad is involved. The problem is solved only in the final, lethal shoot-out.

DEAD RECKONING

George Douglas

After a large-scale post office robbery, expert peterman Edgar Mulley's fingerprints are found on a safe and he lands in jail. The money has never been recovered, and three years later Mulley makes a successful break for freedom. The North Central Regional Crime Squad lands the case when a 'grasser' gets information to them. But before Chief Superintendent Hallam and Inspector 'Jack' Spratt can interrogate the informer, he is found dead. Then, a second mysterious death occurs . . .

THE SILENT INFORMER

P. A. Foxall

A man found murdered in a quiet street brings the police a crop of unpleasant problems. But when the victim is found to have a criminal record, an affluent lifestyle, and no visible honest means of support, the problems proliferate. It seems there could be a lot of villains who wanted him dead. The Catford detectives suddenly find themselves immersed in new enquiries into apparently unrelated crimes of two years ago, which can now be seen to add up to a murderous conspiracy.

DEATH THROWS NO SHADOW

Leo Grex

Mike Capper, a Fleet Street freelance, is after Baroness Rorthy's incredible personal story. However, after making a surprise rendezvous with her, he finds himself confronted by the notorious Andy Beecham, whose Casino Palace is London's latest fashionable fun-spot. Chief Superintendent Gary Bull and Inspector Bert Whitelaw are brought into a mystery which is attended by menace and murder. They uncover a scheme by villains to make use of North Sea oil for a purpose not included in the oil men's plans.